"What the hell are you doing?"

"I'm kidnapping you. Once the bomber realizes you're not dead, we lose the upper hand." He pointed to her jacket with the barrel of the gun. "Toss your sidearm. Please."

"Do you honestly expect me to leave him here?" Digging beneath the leather, she tossed her handgun to the floor.

"Of course not. Rescue is already on the way." He kicked the weapon out of her reach and motioned her to her feet. "Head for the garage."

"You should shoot me now because I'm sure as hell going to shoot you when I get the chance." She rose slowly, expression controlled, voice dropping into dangerous territory. Her eyes narrowed on him. Exhaustion—maybe a bit of pain from the blast— broke through her movements as she stepped around the unconscious forensics expert at her feet.

"Wouldn't expect anything less from you, Sprinkles." The muscles in Braxton's arms and neck tensed. In the thousands of times he'd imagined this moment, this wasn't how he'd expected their reunion to turn out. But there was a killer on the loose, and he wasn't about to lose her again. Not Liz. And not their baby.

RULES IN
DECEIT

NICHOLE SEVERN

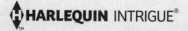

HARLEQUIN INTRIGUE®

To my Bat Signal group, this book never would've gotten finished—twice—without you.

ISBN-13: 978-1-335-64121-2

Rules in Deceit

Copyright © 2019 by Natascha Jaffa

Printed in U.S.A.

www.Harlequin.com

Nichole Severn writes explosive romantic suspense with strong heroines, heroes who dare challenge them and a hell of a lot of guns. She resides with her very supportive and patient husband, as well as her demon spawn, in Utah. When she's not writing, she's constantly injuring herself running, rock climbing, practicing yoga and snowboarding. She loves hearing from readers through her website, www.nicholesevern.com, and on Twitter, @nicholesevern.

Books by Nichole Severn

Harlequin Intrigue

Rules in Blackmail
Rules in Rescue
Rules in Deceit

Visit the Author Profile page at Harlequin.com.

CAST OF CHARACTERS

Elizabeth Dawson—As a former consultant for the NSA and Blackhawk Security's current network analyst, she's capable of building or destroying lives with the touch of a button, but uncovering who wants her dead is out of her depth. And partnering with the man who destroyed her career and her trust may prove fatal to them both.

Braxton Levitt—The former intelligence analyst isn't the traitor Liz believes, but the evidence against him is irrefutable. Fighting to set things right between them will cost him his freedom, but with Liz's life in danger and her program out in the open, he's willing to take the risk. Only, Liz's sealed heart has become more impenetrable than ever.

Sullivan Bishop—Founder and CEO of Blackhawk Security. Former navy SEAL determined to help those local law enforcement can't or won't by recruiting the best operatives in their fields.

Vincent Kalani—Blackhawk Security's forensics expert.

Justin Valentin—CIA agent with deep connections with an extremist group in the Middle East, killed in action due to an error inside the facial recognition program Liz created for the NSA.

Chapter One

"You're not dead." Rage and relief urged Elizabeth Dawson to push away from the conference room table and tackle her former partner to the floor, but she held her control.

"It's good to see you, too, Sprinkles." Braxton Levitt's rich, seductive voice skittered under her skin. The sound of his handpicked nickname for her on his lips—as if they were still friends—tightened the muscles down her spine. That gray gaze pinned her against the back of her chair. A rare occasion. His eyes were normally green, depending on what he wore. She pushed the useless fact to the back of her mind as he planted his elbows on the massive wood table, leaning forward. Thick muscle and tendons flexed beneath his thin T-shirt, and goose bumps prickled down her arms. After all this time, did he honestly think he could walk back into her life after what he'd done?

"Don't call me that." No matter how many times she'd imagined this moment—of confronting him after all these months—there'd always been a small part of grief lodged in her chest. Her fingers curled into the center of her palms beneath the table. She had to stay in control. He wasn't the man she thought he'd been. Her heartbeat pounded loud behind her ears. Something alive—full of fury—clawed its way up her throat, but she couldn't touch him. Not in any way that counted. He'd made damn sure of that when she'd been pulled into countless interrogations after his disappearance. He cost her a career she'd spent a decade building. Now, no one but Blackhawk Security would hire her. Too much of a risk. Elizabeth mirrored his movements, clasping her hands in front of her on top of the table. "You paid my boss for my time, so get on with it. What do you want, Braxton?"

Despite the federal charges stacked against him, Braxton leaned back in his chair as he ran one hand through his dark shoulder-length hair, completely at ease. No longer was he the clean-cut, out-of-shape intelligence analyst she'd known back at the NSA. He'd changed, now something more primal, as though he'd seen things he couldn't possibly forget. New, bulky muscle stretched against the seams in his clothing. Physically different, yet the same man reflected underneath the confidence in his eyes, in his heart-stopping, manipulative smile. Under all those changes, he was still the man who'd walked out on her.

"I missed you." Stubble ran along his jawline, a little fuller than she remembered, deepening the permanent laugh lines around his mouth. She'd once missed the effects of that smile, the gut-clenching delirium he brought to the surface from no more than the upward tilt of his lips. The trust. Scary what that smile could hide.

"Is that why you're here?" she asked. "Because you missed me?"

The blue ball cap pulled low over his head failed to hide the bottom of a scar cut through his left eyebrow he'd gotten during a fight as a teenager. He studied the dark, rainy view of the Chugach mountain range through the floor-to-ceiling windows as if her words hadn't registered then recentered on her. He tapped his fingers against the gleaming conference room table as he sat back in his chair. "No." His shoulders rose on a deep inhale. "Dalton Meyer is dead. Someone tied your old NSA supervisor to a chair and tortured him so they could hijack Oversight and find you. I'm here to make sure that doesn't happen."

Elizabeth's blood iced. "That's not possible."

The facial-recognition program she'd been contracted to build for the NSA had the highest level of security ever coded. She'd designed the system to run autonomously. No human interference. Not even the director of the NSA had access. Its job was to strictly surveil the American population to identify threats to national security using security cameras, traffic cameras, email scanning. Law enforcement, FBI, CIA—they all relied on those feeds. If they'd gone off-line or been hijacked as Braxton suggested...the possibilities were endless.

The threats were endless.

Elizabeth released the breath she'd been holding. There was only one other person in the world who had the ability to override Oversight's programming. And he sat across the table from her. "How did you find me?"

"The fact I'm sitting here says a simple name change isn't working for you, Sprinkles," he said. "If I was able to find you in less than twenty-four hours, how long do you think it'll take someone who's hijacked your program and is gunning for you?"

"Stop calling me that. We're not friends anymore." Her jaw tightened. She followed passing movement outside the conference room through the blinds. Blackhawk Security provided home security, protection and investigative services and handled military contracts. She'd left the NSA behind, left that life behind. She'd moved on. Whatever this was, whatever Braxton wanted from her... No. Protecting her clients was her life now. Sullivan Bishop, Blackhawk Security's founder and CEO, and the rest of the team had taken a chance on her. Trained her without questions about her past. She wasn't about to blow it based on some wild theory the man who'd turned on her had cooked up to come back into her life. If someone had tortured her former project supervisor and was using her own program to hunt her, she had an entire team she could count on now. Former SEALs, Rangers, con men, a profiler. She didn't need him.

"Is that all you thought we were? Friends?" Braxton studied her, staring up at her from below thick, dark eyebrows. "I remember that night, Liz. Hard to believe I was that easy to forget."

"I haven't forgotten anything." She fought against the urge to swipe her hand across her lower abdomen. She'd waited four long months for this moment. Time to get it over with. Time to move on from him. "Since you've brought up that night, you should know I've been trying to find you for a few weeks now to tell you I'm pregnant."

Braxton sat forward in his chair, staring at her from across the table. "H-how?"

Really? That was the question he wanted her to answer? "You want me to explain to you how a woman gets pregnant? Okay. You see, when a woman thinks she's in love with her best friend she's trusted for years—"

"That's not what I meant." He exhaled hard. "We were careful. We used protection."

"Yes, well, obviously that didn't work." The pressure of his full attention tightened her insides. Liquid fire burned through her. She swallowed hard against the sensation. He wasn't supposed to affect her like this. Her crush had ended the night he'd left her to pick up the pieces of his mess. He exuded confidence with his subtle movements. The haze clouding her head dissipated, and she forced everything inside her to go cold as she stood. Digging for her phone, she swiped her thumb across the screen and set the timer. "Now, if you came here for my help, you're out of luck. I don't work for the NSA anymore. So I hope you've got your money's worth. This meeting is over. I'll give you a ten-minute head start before I call the FBI."

"You're being hunted, and you just told me you're pregnant with my baby." Braxton pushed away from the table. Three distinct lines deepened at the bridge of his nose. A day's worth of dark stubble that matched his hair shifted over his strong jaw. "I'm not going anywhere."

"I bet all the girls fall for that line. And, to be fair, I tried to tell you before now, but I couldn't find you." Elizabeth reached for the large oak door. Her instincts screamed for her to put as much space between them as she could. Her muscles had tensed so hard she ached. What did he expect her to do? Take him at his word that he was here to protect her? That he didn't need something from her? Not happening. She flashed her phone's screen at him. "Nine minutes. You're wasting time, Braxton."

He moved fast. Faster than she thought possible. His rough hands pressed into the door, hiking her blood pressure higher as he caged her in the circle of his massive arms. The faint scent of soap and his own masculine scent filled the air, urging her to breathe him in deeper. Two years as coworkers. He'd recruited her for the NSA, helped her land the contract of her career. Taken her to his bed.

"I'm the only one who can protect you, Liz. You know that," he said.

Fury built behind her sternum. A deadly wrath that couldn't be contained anymore.

"How would I know that?" Only the pounding of her heart working overtime filled her ears as she leveled her chin with the floor. She'd been naive to think anything could work between them. Elizabeth fisted her hands at her sides to control the trembling raking through her. She'd trusted him to the end. Denied the allegations the NSA had thrown at her in those interrogations after he vanished.

Braxton Levitt had an entire arsenal of body language, stories and personalities to force his marks into believing he was who he claimed. That was all she was to him. All she had been to him. A mark. "Everything I knew about you turned out to be a lie."

He straightened but kept her caged against the door. "I never lied to you."

"Really? Up until four months ago, I thought we knew everything about each other. You recruited me for the NSA to build Oversight, became the only person I could trust, then took me to your bed, and that same night, you disappeared." The last word hissed from her mouth. She lowered her voice in case the doors weren't soundproofed. "Now you're here, asking me to trust you with my life?" Elizabeth stepped into him, his clean scent surrounding her. It took everything she had—every last reserve of energy—to keep her control in place. "I don't know a damn thing about you, Braxton. I don't think I ever did. Now, let me go before I find a reason to reach for my gun."

His expression fell as he stepped back, taking his body heat with him. "I would never hurt you."

Her heart jolted in her chest from the sincerity in his voice. She studied him with a new mind-set. No emotion. No ties back to the past. Not as a spurned one-night stand but as an operative of Blackhawk Security. The creases around his mouth and the hollow circles under his eyes revealed the exhaustion he'd been dealing with since his disappearance. Worry lines, perhaps? A man on the run certainly became paranoid once stepping back into the spotlight. Every federal organization in the country had searched high and low for him since his disappearance. How had he managed to stay under the radar all this time? Whom had he relied on for help?

Not her. She locked her back teeth together. Didn't matter. This was the last time they'd be in the same room together. He'd slide back under the radar, and she'd go back to doing what she did best: protecting herself—and their baby. She wasn't heartless. She'd just taught herself how to use her heart less. Elizabeth's short black hair slid out from behind her ears as she wrenched the door open. "You already have."

A deep rumble reached her ears, claiming her attention a split second before Braxton shoved her into the hallway, and an eight-foot solid oak door rocketed into her.

BRAXTON LEVITT SLAMMED face-first into the nearest wall. Heat tunneled through his clothing as glass rained down around him. Emergency lighting cast the entire floor into shades of red as alarms kept rhythm with his pulse. He shifted his weight into his hands, flexing his jaw against the pain spreading through his ribs. Something wet slid down his cheek. He swiped at it as a gust of cold Alaskan air and rain rushed through what used to be an entire wall of windows. Blood.

"Liz!" Squinting through the rising smoke, he shoved to his feet. He blinked as a wave of dizziness tipped him into a fern still standing beside the one unhinged door. Yells punctured through the ringing in his ears. The sprinkler system fought to drench the sporadic fires clinging to the walls and the remains of the conference table. He stumbled through what was left of the massive door frame. "You better be alive."

Pain seared through his rib cage. His temples throbbed in rhythm to the alarms. She had to be alive. If he lost her again... No. He couldn't go there. Couldn't think like that. A dull ringing filled his ears. Then a moan. *Her* moan. Braxton's insides burned with an energy he'd learned to contain. A pair of familiar black boots registered in his peripheral vision. "Liz."

Air stalled in his lungs. Not because he'd nearly died in the timed explosion but because for thirty horrible, mind-numbing seconds, he'd lost her all over again. The hollowness of four months and ten days' separation from her vanished as he hauled an oak door and a few other pieces of debris off her with a guttural groan.

Brushing her hair out of her face, he lifted her into him, and the rest of the world fell away. Lean muscle flexed beneath her black leggings and leather jacket as her hand moved to her lower abdomen. Flames crackled around them, sirens already echoing off the surrounding buildings in the street below, but he didn't give a damn. His body's response to Liz had always been off the charts. She'd been the only woman who could make him lose control. Still was. Black smudges highlighted the sharp edges of her cheekbones and jawline. The steady thump at the base of her throat relieved the pressure in his chest, but that relief didn't last long. The bastard who'd hijacked Oversight had set a bomb—for Liz. He was sure of it. That rumbling sound right before the explosion? Had to have been a cell phone on vibrate. A detonator. He should've known the SOB hunting her would've tried to get to her at work. The more casualties, the better chance he had of getting away with murder. More time, more evidence to sift through. Braxton fought the rage spreading rampant beneath his sternum. "Come on, baby, open your eyes. Can you hear me?"

"For once in your life, call me by my actual name." A cough ripped up her throat. She jerked in his arms. Once. Twice. Brown eyes, as dark as chocolate, focused on him. "You do remember what it is, don't you?"

A smile fought for release. He'd missed her fire. Her attitude. Missed her. They'd been a great team back in Fort Meade. Saving the country one line of code at a time. Back before he'd destroyed everything between them to keep her safe. The smile disappeared. None of that mattered now. Keeping her alive—that was all that mattered.

"We've got to go." They had to get out of here before whoever had set that bomb realized he hadn't killed his target. Her lavender-scented shampoo invigorated his senses as she wrapped both arms around him, raising goose bumps on the back of his neck. It'd been a long time since he'd breathed her in. He tightened his hold around her waist. Get her to safety. Find the man using her own program to kill her. Maybe convince her he wasn't the man she believed.

"Liz!" Blackhawk Security's founder and CEO, Sullivan Bishop, shielded his face from the flames as he ran toward them. Braxton had done his homework. He knew the former SEAL had a woman of his own—a JAG Corps prosecutor—but the use of one of his nicknames for her still grated on Braxton's nerves. Liz didn't let anyone give her a nickname. The two had obviously gotten close since she'd relocated to Anchorage, and his gut tightened in response. One of the other operatives followed close on Sullivan's heels. Blackhawk's disgraced NYPD officer, Vincent Kalani, studied the scene, ready for battle. "You all right?"

"I'm fine." Liz wrenched out of Braxton's

grasp, struggling to her feet on her own, all contact between them severed. She brushed debris from her clothing and huffed a piece of hair out of her face. From the outside, it was such an innocent movement, but Braxton understood her tells. He always had. Despite her hard exterior, she'd been rattled. And with good reason. Someone had tried to kill her. But she refused to allow anyone to see vulnerability, especially those she worked with. "But I think it's safe to say our conference room is not. Was anybody hurt in the explosion?"

"No fatalities. From what we can tell, most suffered only minor burns and scrapes from the blast." The forensics expert—Vincent—checked a gash on his forearm, swiping the blood away against his long-sleeve shirt. The muscled, tattooed Hawaiian ran a hand through his shoulder-length brown hair. "Was anyone else in the conference room with you?"

Liz shook her head. "No. Just the two of us."

"Good. As much as I'd like to scour through debris for evidence of who attacked us, let's get to the street. Then you tell me who the hell detonated a bomb in my building." Sullivan turned down the long hallway leading past several now-empty offices, a med clinic and the elevators and stairwell.

"Whoever it was targeted Liz," Braxton said.

Liz rounded into his vision. "There's no evidence proving that bomb was meant for me."

Sullivan twisted around, lips thin, hands ready to tear into the person responsible. "You used to work for the NSA, right? Sold classified intel and disappeared?" The CEO closed the distance between them, expression hard, calculating. "How do I know it wasn't you who set a bomb in my conference room? Some sick game to get Elizabeth back in your life."

"I'd kill any one of you before I let something happen to her. Is that a good enough answer for you?" Braxton straightened, surveying Vincent's position in case the ex-cop made a move, then centered on Sullivan again. "The only thing that matters is this guy is going to keep gunning for her. I'm not going to let that happen."

"Let's move out." Sullivan didn't take his attention off Braxton. "I don't trust you, Levitt." Veins pulsed under the skin of the CEO's arms as he pointed a dirt-smudged finger at him. "If anything happens to her, I will find you, understand?"

"I get that a lot." Despite the threat, Braxton didn't take offense. Liz had an entire team watching her back. He couldn't fault the former Navy SEAL for protecting a member in his unit.

Vincent rounded behind him and Liz to take up the rear with silent obedience.

The sirens grew louder. First responders had arrived on the scene.

But Braxton didn't move. The bomber hadn't attacked Blackhawk Security. Not directly. The bastard had had only one target in mind, and he was staring right at her. The bomb was just the beginning. Whoever had set it would try again as soon as they realized Liz had survived. And what better way to ensure a target had been killed than enter the building as an EMT or firefighter for confirmation? Braxton lowered his voice, instincts prickling. There was more at stake now. They had a baby to consider. He shifted closer to her, pain radiating at the base of his skull as they made their way down the hallway, and lowered his voice to prevent the security cameras from picking up their conversation. "Listen to me, Liz. We can't go to the street."

"Wow, you do remember my name." Liz moved to follow her colleagues.

He threaded his fingers around her arm and pulled her to a stop, holding her against him. The small fires burning around them had nothing on her body heat tunneling through his clothing right then. He covered his mouth and nose in the crook of his arm. "The garage. The only way in is with a key card, right? One exit? He'll expect us down on the street with the others. Not exiting the garage."

"What are you talking about?" She wrenched away from him as though his touch had burned her, his fingertips tingling from the friction against her jacket. Those dark brown eyes locked on him. One second. Two. Wisps of her uneven exhales tickled the oversensitized skin along his neck as she turned on him. "You're insane if you think I'm going anywhere with you."

Damn her stubbornness. One day it was going to get her killed. And then where would he be? He couldn't find the bastard hunting her down without her. No matter how many times he'd tried to keep his distance, every road, every move to stay off the Feds' radar had led him to Anchorage…to her. He didn't care that her program might've already recognized him and reported his location to the

NSA. He wasn't going to leave her unprotected again.

The floor rumbled underneath his feet. The explosion had most likely damaged the building's structure. They didn't have a whole lot of time.

"We need to get moving." Vincent stepped toward them as Blackhawk Security's CEO disappeared into a cloud of smoke toward the stairwell. Close enough for Braxton to reach out and touch him.

He didn't want to have to do this, but the hard determination in Liz's gaze said he didn't have any other choice. "All right. If you're not going to come with me willingly—" Braxton spun, wrapping his grip around the Sig Sauer in Vincent's shoulder holster, and twisted the weapon out of the cop's reach. With one hard swing of the butt of the gun to the operative's head, Vincent went down. Hard. Braxton hefted the gun up, attention leveled on the shocked woman in front of him.

Liz lunged for the unconscious operative. "What the hell are you doing?"

"I'm kidnapping you. Once the bomber realizes you're not dead, we lose the upper hand." He pointed to her jacket with the barrel of the gun. "Toss your sidearm. Please."

"Do you honestly expect me to leave him here?" Digging beneath the leather, she tossed her handgun to the floor.

"Of course not. Rescue is already on the way." He kicked the weapon out of her reach and motioned her to her feet. "Head for the garage."

"You should shoot me now, because I'm sure as hell going to shoot you when I get the chance." She rose slowly, expression controlled, voice dropping into dangerous territory. Her almond-shaped eyes narrowed on him. Exhaustion—maybe a bit of pain from the blast—broke through her movements as she stepped around the unconscious forensics expert at her feet.

"Wouldn't expect anything less from you." The muscles in Braxton's arms and neck tensed. In the thousands of times he'd imagined this moment, this wasn't how he'd expected their reunion to turn out. But there was a killer on the loose, and he wasn't about to lose her again. Not Liz. And not their baby. She shifted in front of him. Every second she stayed out in the open notched his blood pressure higher. "I'm trying to save your life, damn it. Trust me."

"Stop asking me to trust you." Liz headed

for the stairwell, fire reflecting in her dark gaze. "I'm still trying to get over the last time you betrayed me."

Chapter Two

A wall of cold slammed into Elizabeth as they hit the parking garage. Only a handful of Blackhawk Security vehicles waited in their assigned spaces. There was no mysterious bomber waiting to ambush them as Braxton had suggested upstairs, but the illusion of safety never settled.

Could have had something to do with the fact the man she'd thought she'd loved all those months ago—the man whose child she carried—had a gun pressed against her spine. Smoke still registered on the air, the flashing of emergency lights bouncing off the cement walls from the street. There were only two ways out of the garage, and a bomb had taken out one of them. The other was the gate leading to the street, but she didn't reach for the key card all operatives were required to carry. And she wouldn't. Not until she had some answers. Scanning the SUVs, Elizabeth stopped dead in her tracks. "What's the plan now?"

"Now we get out of here." Braxton pressed his hand into the small of her back, bringing her into his side as he moved them toward one of the SUVs. His natural scent wrapped around her, but she didn't find comfort there like she used to. "Don't suppose you brought a set of car keys?"

"Must've left them in the jacket that doesn't smell like smoke." Pain washed through her. She glanced down at the gun aimed into her rib cage then quickly back to their surroundings as they closed in on the nearest SUV. Safety still on. Interesting. Sweat dripped down her spine as rain struck the cement at the edges of the asphalt. Him coming back here, the explosion… Her pulse throbbed at the base of her skull. This was insane. That bomb could've been meant for any operative on the team. For all she knew, it could've been meant for him. So why come back? Blackhawk Security wasn't in the habit of filling in the authorities on their clients, but her boss should've made an exception for Braxton Levitt. The NSA wouldn't stop looking for him. He'd never be a free man as long as treason charges were on the table. "What makes you think whoever set that bomb is targeting me?"

"Someone tortured your project supervisor and hijacked Oversight." He kept his attention on the prize ahead, occasionally studying their surroundings as they moved. Ten feet until they reached the nearest SUV. His expression tightened beneath the shadows cast from the baseball cap. "Call it instinct."

"Tell me you're joking." Elizabeth ripped away from his touch and shoved him away. He wouldn't use the gun on her. This entire kidnapping was a charade. "That's not enough evidence to insert yourself back into my life. You left, Braxton. You lost the right to pretend you care about anybody other than yourself."

The green-gray eyes she'd been trying to forget for the last four months locked on her, those mountainous shoulders deflating beneath his heavy brown jacket. "Liz—"

The stairwell door slammed closed behind them. Braxton twisted back over his shoulder, hefting the gun up and over toward the imagined threat. He stepped in front of her as though he intended to protect her from harm. But he wasn't a protector. No matter how many times he claimed he'd come back to keep her safe.

Thrusting her knee into the back of his, Elizabeth pushed him forward. The gun dropped to the pavement, metal on asphalt loud in her ears as he fought to balance. Lunging for it, she barely wrapped her fingers around the grip before he pulled her upright, his grip on her wrist cutting off circulation. Damn, he moved fast.

His breath fanned across the sensitive skin along her collarbones. Warmth spread from her neck up into her cheeks as he held her close, his mouth mere centimeters from hers. A mouth meant for spilling lies. "I'm not here to hurt you, Liz. I would never hurt you."

Did she really have to remind him there were more ways to hurt her than the physical? He'd destroyed her career, gotten her pregnant and disappeared. It wasn't until Sullivan Bishop and the Blackhawk Security team had offered her a place as their network security analyst three months ago that she'd started pulling the shattered pieces of her life back together. Without them, who knew where she would be right now.

"Let me go." She fought to free herself, but Braxton only held her tighter. Once upon a time, she would've enjoyed that strong grip around her. Her insides instantly clenched. Now, the only thought running through her head centered on getting as far from him as possible. "What do you want from me?"

Her hand shook around the warm steel of the gun. She couldn't let him get inside her head.

"I want you alive, for starters." He pressed her against him, his fingertips leaving impressions in the small of her back. He studied her from forehead to chin. "If that means I have to knock you unconscious and throw you over my shoulder, I will."

Air rushed from her lungs. The sincerity in his gaze, in his voice... He meant it. A short burst from one of the police sirens tensed the muscles down her spine but brought her back into the moment. "You actually believe someone is trying to kill me?"

"I have the proof." Braxton released his hold on her wrist but let her keep the gun. Offering her a hand, he gave her the space to make the choice for herself. "All you have to do is trust me."

"You make it sound so easy." Every cell in her body urged her to take his hand. The sharp angles to his jaw, the heavy five o'clock shadow, the slight bend in his nose where he'd broken it playing football one summer, even the thin slice of scar across his palm where he'd slipped on ice in elementary school... It was all so familiar. Comforting. But she didn't know this man. The Braxton she'd known never would've deserted her in the first place.

She forced her attention to his eyes. "If I agree to go with you, you will answer every question I have."

"I give you my word." His voice dropped an octave. Sensual, compelling.

Her chest tightened on a deep inhale. She loosened her grip around the gun, the tingling sensation in her fingers subsiding as she leveled her chin with the asphalt. Handing over Vincent's stolen Sig Sauer, Elizabeth drew back when his fingers closed on top of hers. In an almost militaristic manner, he cleared the loaded round, dropped the magazine, slammed it back into place and chambered another. No. Whoever stood in front of her wasn't *her* Braxton. This man was hardened, muscled. Dangerous. She exhaled against the nausea churning inside. "And when this is over, you'll crawl back to the rock you've been hiding under for the last four months. Are we clear?"

The lines etched between his dark eyebrows deepened. He dropped the gun to his side, so casual she'd believe he'd handled a firearm all his life. Which wasn't the case. "Do you remember what I said to you that first day we met?"

The words forced their way forward from the back of her mind. Her throat tightened around the memory of her first day of working for the NSA, the day she'd met him. She swiped her tongue across her dry lips. "I sat down at the desk next to yours with my ice cream from the cafeteria, and you made fun of my choice of topping." Rainbow-colored sprinkles. The nickname he'd called her ever since. A smile pulled at one edge of her mouth. "Then you said, 'One thing you need to understand here, Sprinkles. This place will eat you alive. Stick with me, and no matter what happens, you can count on me to get you out of it.'" A hint of smoke coming off his clothing singed deep into her lungs as she focused on him. "And I believed you."

"Do you still believe me?" he asked.

Yes. No. Her stomach flipped. If someone was trying to kill her, she wouldn't stand around here all day waiting for it to happen. "I don't know what to believe."

Movement registered in her peripheral vision at the automatic gate. A firefighter. He'd presumably been assigned to check the rest of the building for signs of structural damage and flames. Dressed in full protective equipment, including face shield, he stopped just outside the gate and tried to pull it up manually. Wouldn't work. That gate didn't open for anybody unless they worked in the building.

He'd have to get the fire code from her boss, Sullivan Bishop. Stiffness drained from the muscles around her spine a split second before the gate lifted on its own. "Everything okay down here?"

Braxton turned, maneuvering the gun behind his back. Out of sight.

"We're fine. How'd you get in? That gate is supposed to be sealed." Warning bells rang loud in her head. That wasn't right. Nobody could access that gate—not even emergency personnel—without a Blackhawk Security operative key card or individualized code. She dropped her voice as the firefighter advanced. Too fast. Alone. "Braxton…"

The firefighter lifted a handgun and took aim. At her.

A strong hand pushed her to the ground as a bullet ripped past her ear. The garage turned on its axis. Braxton took position in front of her as he returned fire. Pain shot up through her knees, loose asphalt ripping holes in her leggings, but Elizabeth didn't hesitate. Digging in her jacket pocket, she wrapped her hand around the keys to her company SUV near the shooter and hit the panic button.

Headlights flashed; the alarm blared. It'd only distract the shooter for a few seconds, but that was all she needed. The gunfire died.

She shoved to her feet and sprinted for Elliot Dunham's SUV. Blackhawk Security's private investigator usually left his keys in the front seat, and she silently prayed he hadn't changed up his routine. "Come on!"

Footsteps echoed close behind her as bullets two and three barely missed their mark. Chunks of cement nicked at her exposed skin, and she raised her arms to protect her face. Wouldn't do a damn bit of good against a bullet, but instinct and adrenaline drove her now. She rounded the tail end of Elliot's SUV and wrenched the door open. No keys. She dived inside, ripping the visor down. The keys dropped into her lap.

Braxton took cover behind the hood, squeezing off another shot. Then a third.

"Get in!" Elizabeth pulled the driver's side door closed and started the engine. Shoving the SUV into Drive, she paused as the shooter positioned himself directly in front of them.

Hiking himself into the back seat, Braxton tapped on her shoulder. "Liz, go!"

The firefighter raised his gun, taking aim. One second. Two. And fired.

She froze as the bulletproof glass held against the shot. Then unfroze as rage coursed through her. The shooter had come for *her*, targeted *her*. Lifting her foot from the brake, she slammed on the accelerator and steered directly into the shooter. The growl of the engine drowned the pounding of her heartbeat in her ears. Pressure built in her lungs. "Hang on back there."

Her leather seat protested against his grip on the headrest. "Liz…"

The shooter pulled the trigger two more times, each bullet caught in the windshield, a split second before he launched himself out of the way of the vehicle.

Elizabeth spun the steering wheel toward the still-open security gate. Bouncing in her seat as they catapulted over the gate's tracks, she fishtailed out of the garage. Blackhawk Security grew distant in the rearview mirror. Two familiar faces stepped into the middle of the road behind them, but she didn't have time to stop and explain everything to her team. Braxton had been telling the truth.

Someone was targeting her, but she wasn't the only one she had to worry about now. She lifted her gaze to the rearview mirror, to the father of her unborn baby. "Fine. You can take me to whatever safe house you've set up until we figure out who you think is trying to kill me. But to be clear, it's not because I trust you." Elizabeth took a deep breath, her ribs aching from the explosion in the conference room, then forced her attention back to the road. "It's because you got me pregnant."

"I STILL CAN'T believe it." Braxton couldn't think. Couldn't breathe. Someone had tried to kill the woman he vowed to protect, but it was more than that. Adrenaline drained from his veins in small increments, but not enough to clear his head.

Wow. Liz was pregnant. And he was the father. She'd told him before the explosion, but he hadn't been able to process that until now. It'd been kind of hard to think when the bullets were flying. Reaction—that was what he was good at. But…he was going to be a father. A smile threatened to overwhelm his features, pure joy exploding through him.

"Someone just tried to kill us. Twice. Can we please focus on that?" The weight of her attention pinned him against his seat from the rearview mirror. "I think we have bigger problems to talk about."

"I think the fact you're pregnant is pretty big." He swayed with the SUV as she wound through neighborhoods, around strip malls and into the edges of the city. Days of staying off the grid, months of grueling physical training, years of working for the NSA… none of it had prepared him for this. A baby.

He compressed the safety button on the stolen gun and set it beside him on the seat. They were going to have a baby. "Might as well not have used protection at all."

"Yeah, apparently, latex wasn't strong enough for your swimmers." A hint of a smile played across her mouth, the first softening of her guard since he set sights on her in the conference room. "If you're thinking about asking me whether or not I'm sure the baby is yours, I'll save you the time. Yes, Braxton, she's yours. No, Braxton, I haven't been with anybody else since the night you took me to bed then disappeared without a word. And, yes, I'm keeping the baby. I plan to raise her on my own without help. Any other questions?"

"It's a girl?" He ran his palms over the baseball cap and interlaced his fingers at the crown of his head. He turned away from her, surveying the curve of the street but not really seeing where they were. The muscles across his back strained under the self-induced pressure. He didn't know what else to say, what to think. They were having a girl?

"I found out the sex a couple days ago." The vulnerability in her voice compelled him to face her again, but she'd turned her gaze back to the road. Snow and ice kicked up along the

SUV. She rolled her lips between her teeth. "This wasn't how I wanted you to find out. I tried to find you, but four months is a long time waiting for you to come back. Figured you'd moved on and I could do the same. When I got tired of the NSA interrogating me about your whereabouts, I changed my name in every federal database I could hack and relocated."

He'd known about her search effort but ultimately decided to stay away. It'd been the hardest decision of his life and the only way to keep her safe. Until four days ago when he'd learned about Dalton Meyer's murder and that Oversight's feeds had been hacked. Until he'd uncovered the program's surveillance logs. Someone had put her in their crosshairs.

Intense pressure built behind his sternum as she took a sharp left. The city came into focus for the first time since Braxton had gotten in the vehicle. A familiar line of bare trees surrounding Fairview Lions Park cut off his air. A good foot of snow covered the all-too-familiar horseshoe pit and most of the green and purple playground where he'd spent countless nights as a kid after his father had lost the house to the bank. Right there, under the small rock wall. He forced his attention back to the rearview mirror as a group of homeless made their way down the street, back to her, his anchor. No point in studying the weathered faces as they passed. His old man had most likely died from his addictions a long time ago. Wasn't important. The past was dead, and he sure as hell would make sure it stayed that way. "Did you also figure moving here was enough to keep me from finding you?"

"I'd accepted you weren't coming back." Liz cocked her head. "In retrospect, I guess Anchorage had been on my mind since you told me you'd never step foot in this city again. It'd worked until an hour ago." She glanced at him—almost too fast for him to catch it—then back to the road. "You never told me how you managed to find me."

"You're predictable. I knew you'd never change your first name." Not after what she'd told him about her mother and the long line of Elizabeths in her family. "As for your new last name, I remembered your favorite TV show growing up. Wasn't hard to sift through the short list of Elizabeth Dawsons and track you down from there."

Nothing would've stopped him from finding her.

"I'll keep that in mind next time." Her knuckles tightened over the steering wheel.

There wouldn't be a next time. Not if he had anything to say about it. She turned the SUV east, leaving the park and memories he'd worked hard to bury behind. "So are you going to tell me where this safe house of yours is or are we going to drive around all night?"

"Make one more loop around the neighborhood." Braxton studied the cars behind them. They hadn't been followed. Whoever had taken shots at them in the parking garage probably hadn't been able to make it past the wall of police officers and emergency personnel surrounding the building. At least, not in a hurry. On top of that, her team had seen them race from the scene. His pulse hammered at the base of his skull, and he wiped at the dried patches of blood along his forehead. He should've known the bastard would come at her at Blackhawk Security. As far as he'd been able to tell over the last few days, that was where she'd spent most of her time. Day and night. Protecting her clients just as she'd protected millions of lives during her contract work for the NSA. And now with a baby. "Have you told your team?"

"No. Not yet." Her shoulders rose on an audible inhale. Hesitation tightened the cords running down her neck. She made another turn, seemingly refusing to look back at him.

"I was thinking of telling Sullivan about the baby today, but then someone blew up the conference room and it sort of slipped to the back of my mind."

A laugh escaped from his control. She always did have a way of downplaying stressful situations with sarcasm. "Understandable."

"I work in network security now." Liz ran a hand through her hair and levered her elbow against the driver's side door. "My clients come to me to assess their firewalls, encrypt the information on their servers, basically make their networks unhackable. I analyze shell corporations and perform background checks for everyone on my team. I can't think of a single person who would want me dead."

"All I know is someone tried to kill you back there." He wouldn't discount the possibility the threat was tied to Blackhawk Security. They had to consider all the angles. Past, present, someone invested in the outcome of the firm's military and private contracts. The list of suspects with the kind of knowledge and training that shooter had to have was endless, but military training was a definite. He needed access to her client files. "And I'm not going to let them succeed."

"Do you think this could be linked to my contract with the NSA?" Her voice wavered.

To someone who hadn't memorized every inflection, every emotion, it would've gone unnoticed. But not to him. He knew her inside and out, down to a cellular level. Even with filtered moonlight coming through the SUV's tinted windows, he noted the color draining from her face. Hell. The nightmares. How could he have forgotten about her damn nightmares? Her throat worked to swallow. "Maybe a family member or someone who'd gotten a look at the files?"

Her fear slid through him, and his body reacted automatically. Ready for battle to protect what was his. One breath. Two. "You still have nightmares."

Not a question. He was there during Oversight's trial run. He'd witnessed how it'd affected her.

"Assuming the person who shot at us in the garage is the same person who hacked those feeds, which might not be the case, you should be able to use my backdoor access to narrow down a location." Him? Liz twisted the steering wheel to the right a little too hard. He fell back against the seat and reached out for his gun before it fell to the floor. Okay, so she didn't want to talk about what kept her up at night, but he couldn't find this bastard on his own. He needed her to run the program. "The only problem is the access opens a two-way door. The second you lock on to a location, he has yours."

"Don't you mean he'd have *our* location?" he asked.

"No, Braxton." She set her jaw, chancing a quick glance into the rearview mirror. "I told you the day I terminated my consulting contract with the NSA. I'll never touch that program again. If you want to trace those feeds, you're doing it alone."

Braxton didn't answer.

"Turn right at the next street. Third building from the end of the road." The apartment he'd leased under a fake name off one of those online sites where home owners rented out their homes wasn't much. Two bedrooms, two bathrooms. But it would get the job done while he was back in Anchorage. However long that would be. He studied Liz as she pulled the SUV to the curb then shouldered his way out of the vehicle behind her. She stepped onto the pavement, hand supporting her head where shrapnel had cut into her during the explosion. A groan worked up her throat, and his blood pressure spiked. He stepped into her, her rough exhale skimming across his neck as rain pounded onto his shoulders. "You okay?"

"It's nothing." She dropped her hand and

stepped away. Her right hand shook slightly. She tried to hide it by curling her fingers into her palms, but she couldn't hide from him.

She was scared. Rightfully so, but he'd die before he let anything happen to her. Or their baby. "I'm not going to let that bastard lay a finger on you. I promise."

Silence settled between them. Tight, thick and full of distance.

"I only agreed to your help because someone was shooting at us, and I didn't want to die." Liz shook her head. "So I don't need your promises. I need you to keep me alive until I figure out who wants me dead."

Chapter Three

Elizabeth hefted the SUV's gate above her head and lifted the black duffel bag standard for all Blackhawk Security operatives from the dark interior. Mostly supplies. A couple changes of clothes, ammunition, food storage, emergency flares. The basics of her new profession. Never knew what kind of weather or client would come calling. Although they'd borrowed Elliot's SUV, and the clothes weren't going to fit her. "If you're not going to trace Oversight's feeds on your own, fill me in on your plan."

They'd wound a lot of circles through neighborhoods, parks and strip malls, finally ending up at what looked like an apartment complex. The shooter hadn't followed them. She would've spotted him through the maze of routes they'd taken. The SOB who'd taken a shot at her was most likely licking his wounds and devising another way to kill her.

If Braxton had been telling the truth about the shooter's target. She paused at the thought. She took care of network security for a start-up security company. Wasn't exactly the kind of job that would land her in a killer's cross-hairs. But if this had anything to do with her work for the NSA…

No. It couldn't. She'd left that life behind months ago. Besides, those files were classified. It'd take someone with much higher security clearance than the director of the NSA to access them. That'd been part of the deal. She'd signed dozens of nondisclosure agreements about the program's trial run, and the federal government would hide Oversight's existence at all costs.

"First, I want your forensics guy to analyze those bullets in the windshield." Braxton leaned against the back quarter panel mere inches from her, arms crossed across that broad chest of his. The weight of his attention pressurized the air in her lungs. He watched her carefully, as though he couldn't miss a single moment. "Maybe we'll get lucky with an ID on the unsub trying to kill you, and—"

"And you go back into hiding." That was the deal. She'd agreed to his protection, and as soon as they had a viable lead on that shooter, he'd go back to whatever rock he been hiding under for the last four months and let her move on with her life. Alone. Storm clouds shifted overhead as the last remnants of rain pelted against her leather jacket, but the crisp, cleansing atmospheric scent did nothing to clear her head. Unzipping the duffel, she reached in, wrapped her shaking hand around her teammate's backup weapon, and loaded a fresh magazine. Full.

"Right," he said.

Setting the bag back in the trunk, she faced Braxton with her emotions in check and her guard in place. He might be the father of her unborn baby, but that didn't mean she had to trust him. Elizabeth lifted her gaze to his. "You think going back to Blackhawk Security to hand over the bullets is a good idea? I seem to remember half of the penthouse floor is missing, and we almost died in the garage."

Braxton moved in close, too close, his clean, masculine scent mixing with the aroma of rain. The combination urged her to lean into him, to forget how much she'd missed him. She'd told herself—hell, told him—she'd moved on, but her body had yet to grasp the idea. "I told you I won't let him touch you. You have my word."

"And I told you your word doesn't mean a damn thing to me." She fought back a quiver.

Tightness ran down her neck and back. After countless hours—months—of trying to find him, here he stood less than a foot away. In the flesh. Tightening her grip around the duffel bag, she scrambled for purchase as the past threatened to drag her under. No. She'd been down this path once before. She'd trusted him, and it cost her everything. "We should ditch the vehicle and get inside. If the shooter is the same person who hijacked Oversight's feeds, he'll be able to track us to this area and try to shoot me again."

Ten minutes later, they'd abandoned the SUV, sans bullets in the windshield, and hiked back to the apartment on foot. Braxton led her up two flights of stairs and toward an apartment in the back of the third building, his clothing barely concealing the muscle he'd put on since the last time she'd seen him. And not just in his upper body. His legs flexed beneath denim, powerful and strong. Inserting a key in the lock, he turned the doorknob and shouldered the door open. "Wait here a minute."

He didn't wait for her answer as he disappeared inside.

A breeze shook the trees below, and she stepped to the railing. No shooters waiting in the trees. No bomb ticking off nearby. She smoothed her hand over her lower abdomen as a rush of nausea churned in her stomach. Who would want her dead? And why now?

"Surveillance is clean." Braxton filled the door frame just inside her peripheral vision. "The place isn't much, but it gets the job done. We've got power, water, gas, and I had groceries delivered yesterday."

She followed him inside, the skin along her collarbones prickling with the onslaught of a draft coming from the vents above. "Hiding your how-to-be-a-good-spy magazines before I came inside?"

"No, I keep those locked up all the time." Braxton's laugh replaced the cold-induced goose pimples along her arms with heat, but she couldn't afford to give it much notice. Find out who was trying to kill her and why, then move on with her life. That was it.

He'd been right about the apartment. It wasn't much, but it'd work for what they needed. Large windows took up most of the east wall, providing a jaw-dropping view of the mountains. A large sectional had been positioned in the corner of the living room, only photos of wildlife and scenic Alaska hanging on the white walls. Two bedrooms, two bathrooms from the looks of it. Simple. Bare. But the setup of surveillance equipment across the dining room table said secure. It suited him. Her, too.

"You can take the back bedroom if you want to clean up. There's a bathroom attached to that one, so we don't have to share." Braxton maneuvered behind her, and she straightened a bit more. "I'll have some food for us by the time you're done."

"Good idea. Give me a few minutes." She checked her wristwatch. Nine at night. They weren't going to get much done at this hour. The investigation would have to start in the morning. Another rush of nausea gripped her tight, and she fought to breathe through her nose to counter it. Didn't work. The target of a shooter, reunited with the man she thought she'd never see again, and suffering from morning sickness all at the same time. Great.

"Take your time." He headed toward the kitchen, tossing his baseball cap onto the counter. His dark hair skimmed his shoulders, and, hell, she'd be lying if she didn't admit the look worked for him.

Elizabeth forced one foot in front of the other. Space. She needed space. Away from him. The lighttan-colored walls passed in a blur as she escaped to the nearest bedroom. She wasn't sure if this was the room he'd meant for her to take, but at the moment, she didn't care. Tossing her duffel onto the floor, she exhaled hard and ran a hand through her hair.

It'd been four months since she'd made the worst mistake of her life by climbing under the sheets with Braxton. That should've been long enough to get control of her physical reactions. Damn it. This wasn't the plan. She'd accepted there would be a bottomless hole in her heart where she'd shove everything she felt for Braxton Levitt in order to raise their daughter on her own. But he'd come back. To protect her. Still, while she might have to stay within physical proximity of him, she wouldn't let him hurt her again. Keeping her emotional distance would have to do. That, and a securely locked bedroom door. "Just a few days, baby girl. We've got this."

The bedroom came into focus. Single queen-size bed, nightstand, dresser with some papers settled on top, same type of photography on the walls as she'd noticed in the living room. And a cardboard box full of phones stashed in the corner. She fished out a phone from the middle of pile and studied the room again. Groceries delivered, a box of phones, surveillance setup. How long had Braxton planned on staying here?

She swiped her thumb across the screen

and dialed Vincent Kalani's number from memory. She'd left her phone with the SUV about a mile west of here. Anyone who tried pinging it for a location would only find disappointment. Blackhawk Security training 101. The other line rang three times. Then four. "Come on, Vincent. Pick up the phone." Another ring. If he hadn't made it out of the building alive, she'd never forgive herself for leaving the forensics expert in the middle of a crime scene. "Pick up the damn—"

"Kalani." Vincent's usually smooth voice sounded rough, damaged.

"You're alive." Relief flooded through her. She exhaled hard, closing her eyes with a hand on her forehead. Turning her back to the door, she ignored the burn in her lower lash line. Hormones. Crying came too easy these days. "I was beginning to worry I'd be stuck with your vengeful ghost for the rest of my life."

"No thanks to your new bodyguard there." Muffled static reached through his end of the line. "What number are you calling from?"

"A burner I picked up out of a box full of phones. Consider this my new number for the time being." She chewed on the end of her thumbnail. They shouldn't have left him behind. She could've fought Braxton harder, could've done *something.* "Tell me you're okay."

"I'm good," Vincent said. "Confirm you're safe and give me permission to punch your ex in the face the next time I see him."

"I'm safe. For now. And permission granted." She dropped her hand and rolled her shoulders back. Pain shot through the right side of her rib cage, and she doubled over with a rough exhale. "But you'll have to get in line."

"Liz?" Vincent asked. "You okay?"

"Fine for someone who took an eight-foot oak door to the right side." She breathed through the pain. "Listen, whoever set that bomb tried to finish the job in the garage. I pulled three slugs out of Elliot's windshield, but I'm not sure how to hand them off to you without putting myself back in the open."

"Stay put," Vincent said. "I'll have Anchorage PD's crime scene unit check it out. Maybe we'll get lucky on a stray casing. If that doesn't work, we'll set something up to get me those slugs. You should know, as of right now the Sovereign Army is taking credit for the bombing."

"The privacy activists? Explosives aren't usually their forte." Headlines had taken over national news with the group's intent to sell and publish congressmen and women's browsing histories and darkest secrets, but setting a bomb at a security company? Although if the extremist group discovered she'd helped the federal government create a surveillance system to spy on them for the past year, who knew how far they'd escalate. Still, something about that didn't sit well. A knock at the door pushed her pulse higher. Braxton. She nodded, even though Vincent couldn't possibly see it, and turned as the bedroom door cracked open. "Thanks for the intel. Call me if you find anything else."

She ended the call, nervous energy skittering up her spine.

Green-gray eyes locked on her and, suddenly, the last four months disappeared to the back of her mind. Braxton made his way inside, a white box in one hand and a steaming bowl of something intoxicating in the other. "Your team?"

"Yeah. Hope you don't mind I borrowed one of your phones to make the call." She tossed the burner onto the bed, crossing her arms over her midsection. Grinding her teeth, she fought against the pain ripping through her side. "Looks like Sovereign Army took credit for the bombing. Vincent's sending Anchorage PD to analyze the scene in the garage.

He'll call back if he finds something. He's very much looking forward to punching you in the face when he sees you again."

"Fair enough." A smile curled at one edge of his mouth, and his all-too-familiar pull hooked into her. Damn it. When would he stop affecting her like this? Braxton closed the space between them, coming within mere inches of her. Her breath caught in her throat as he maneuvered around her to set the bowl on the nightstand. Straightening, he backed away slowly, that mesmerizing gaze steady on her. "So now that there's nothing more we can do tonight, take off your shirt."

EXPERTS SAID TIME healed old wounds, but what the hell did they know? Braxton popped open the first aid kit beside him on the bed. How many times had he called her over the last month from this very same safe house only to hang up when she answered? Two? Five? Maybe more. She wouldn't have spoken to him if he'd opened his mouth. That was clear now. More than likely, she would've demanded a trace on the call the second she'd realized who was on the other line and sent any resource available his way. His disappearance obviously hadn't torn her apart as much as it had him. But, hell, he deserved it. Even if leaving had been to protect her.

"Excuse me?" Liz cradled her rib cage. Her features contorted but smoothed almost instantly. As though she'd caught herself in a moment of weakness.

Stubborn woman. On a scale from one to ten, he pegged her pain around a seven. Yet she hadn't said a word. He'd noticed the way she favored that side, the small flinches in her expression. She'd been lucky to survive that explosion. If it weren't for the very same oak door that'd possibly cracked her ribs protecting her from most of the shrapnel, she might not be standing here. The ache under his sternum, the one connected with the woman standing mere feet away, refused to subside as he studied the fast tick of her pulse at the base of her throat. "The only way for me to see if your ribs are broken is you taking off your shirt."

"I'm fine. I'm sure it's a rib out of place. It'll either pop back when it's ready, or this girl will kick it back where it belongs in the next few months." She stared up at the ceiling, her fingers prodding into her side. Small lines creased her expression, and his gut clenched. In her next breath, she took back control. "Besides, I'm pretty sure you're just looking for a way back under my shirt. Which isn't going to happen."

A laugh rumbled from deep in his chest. Exhaustion played a wicked game across her expression, but she'd keep going until they identified the unsub responsible for that bomb. That'd been one of the reasons he'd recommended her to Dalton Meyer for the Oversight project at the NSA two years ago. He'd studied her work programming drones for the small start-up company in Washington, DC, and admired her determination to get the job done. Nothing had changed in that respect. But sacrificing her health in the name of the investigation wouldn't get them anywhere. "Can you blame a guy for trying?"

Her burst of laughter filled the room but cut off in her next breath. She doubled over, hiking her hand into her side.

"All right, enough stalling." Braxton tossed the first aid kit onto the bed and propelled himself to his feet. "I'm taking a look at your ribs whether you like it or not."

"Why?" Liz straightened slowly, pain evident on her features. "Unless you got your medical degree while you were in hiding?"

"Not exactly, but you learn a few things when you're on your own and the government has plastered your face on the front page of the FBI's website." He feathered his fingertips under her shirt and lifted the black silk. Her sharp gasp quickened his pulse, and a rush of satisfaction shot through him. He'd always been able to change her breathing patterns with one touch. Nice to know some things hadn't changed. Smooth skin slid against the rough calluses on his hand. And wasn't that the perfect metaphor for their relationship— rough versus smooth. Bruises had already started darkening around her bottom rib on the right side. He studied her expression in his peripheral vision as he pressed his thumb into the bone. "It's no way to live, though. Strange cities, fake names, avoiding human interaction." Avoiding her. "Gets old real fast."

"Well, now it looks like we have something in common." She hissed as he prodded the third rib from the bottom. "Now I'm being hunted like an animal. Only this predator isn't the federal government and has tried to blow me up and shoot me in the same day."

He locked his jaw to cool the anger churning in his gut. If he hadn't left, none of this would've happened.

"Nothing feels broken." Braxton dropped his hand. Every cell in his body screamed for him to erase the worry lines from her expression, but he couldn't move. He studied the vulnerability playing across her face. What he wouldn't give to help her forget the nightmare of the last couple hours. "I'll get you a heating pad for the soreness and ice for the inflammation. Should be good as new in a couple days."

A weak smile played across her mouth. "Thanks."

He turned away from her and headed toward the door. If he didn't, the unquenched desire that'd burrowed itself beneath his skin and crackled along his veins when he touched her would take control. Her life—their baby's life—had been put at risk because of him. Anything more between them would only make it that much harder to walk away. That'd been the deal. She agreed to his protection. He'd go back into hiding. Fighting to keep his focus trained, Braxton forced one foot in front of the other.

"Why'd you come back?" she asked. "Why now?"

He froze, his hands curling into fists at his side. Ten seconds. That was all he needed to clear his head, but she couldn't even give him that. "Liz—"

"I'd finally worked out what I would say to our baby the day she asked about her father, but then you walked right into Blackhawk Security. Have to admit—" she fitted her shirt back into place out of the corner of his eye "—I never saw it coming."

Braxton turned. No point in lying. He'd never been able to stay away from her for more than a few days at a time. Even now, he was caught in the undeniable gravitational pull of hers, and he wouldn't be able to fight it much longer. "I always planned on coming back."

"Did you ever think you never should've left in the first place?" Her expression shifted from genuine curiosity to outright fury. The small muscles along her jaw flexed. Liz took a step back as he approached then brushed right past him. As though his revelation ignited that anger she desperately fought to control. "Maybe then we wouldn't be in this mess."

He wrapped his hand around hers and pulled her into him. Lean muscle flexed along her arm, and he imagined all too easily exploring every inch of the strength under her clothing. Every mole. Every scar. The soft curve of her lower abdominals where their baby thrived. He brushed his thumb over the back of her hand and loosened his grip. Desire surged through him, a mere taste of the chaos capable of rendering him completely useless when she was around. Damn what she thought of him, damn the investigation or the reason he'd stayed away from her for the last sixteen weeks. She had to know the truth. She deserved to know.

Liz stared up at him with that gorgeous fire in her expression—almost daring him to make his next move—but didn't wrench out of his hold.

He forced the words to the tip of his tongue, but no sound left his mouth. Licking his lips, he dropped his hand from hers. No. Now wasn't the time. Because he couldn't lose her again. Every decision he'd made over his career had a price, but he'd never expected her to pay for any of it. And she would once she learned the truth.

"You're right. I never should've left, and I'll spend the rest of my life making it up to you and our baby if that's what you want." He framed her hips between both hands, his thumbs grazing her lower belly. Braxton stepped into her, relishing in the slight widening of her eyes, of her exhale rushing against the skin along his neck. "Starting now."

Reaching past her, he skimmed his hand over the top of the dresser and grabbed the yellow envelope resting on top. He slid it between them and handed it to her. Everything that'd happened today at Blackhawk Security—the bomb, the shooter in the garage—had to do with what was in the envelope. "You asked me why I came back. Why now? This is why."

She took the envelope from him, the furrow between her dark eyebrows deepening. She slid her fingers inside the envelope and pulled out the short stack of surveillance photos he'd collected from Oversight's servers. Photos of her. Confusion deepened the lines across her forehead. "What is this?"

She blinked as realization hit her hard.

He wanted to reach for her. To comfort her. But didn't.

The envelope protested in her hand. Liz shook her head and took a step back. She shuffled through the stack of photos, one after the other. But studying photos wouldn't make the truth any less real. Someone had been hunting her for months. "Wh-how did you get these?"

"I programmed an alert into Oversight's code to notify me when you were the subject before I left the agency." If he hadn't, she—and their baby—wouldn't be standing here right now. "I started getting alerts six days ago. Right after I read about Dalton Meyer's murder and discovered Oversight's feeds were hijacked."

"So many photos. Outside the office, getting into my car." Her voice barely registered. Too soft. Too full of fear. The muscles down his spine responded. She swallowed hard, eyes wide. "This one is from a traffic camera as I drove home." Liz ran a hand through her hair as her mouth parted. "Someone's been watching me? For how long?"

"No, someone has been stalking you." He picked out one particular photo from the back and handed it to her. A photo of her leaving her own home. Whoever had been watching her knew where she lived. "And I'm here to find out why."

Chapter Four

"I don't think the Sovereign Army took these pictures." Elizabeth dropped the photos in her hand to her side. She'd been followed for weeks—maybe months. She'd had no idea, but she couldn't let the fear spreading at the back of her mind take control. What else had her stalker uncovered? Her head spun. Nausea festered. *Focus.* She forced herself to breathe deep. She'd started a new life here, loved her job, was having a baby. Nobody would take that from her. Not some extremist group. Not Braxton. And not whoever had tried to blow her up three hours ago.

She headed for the door. Braxton was a former analyst. Analysts ran secure networks. All she needed was a computer. She trusted her team—trusted Vincent—with her life, but she had to see the Sovereign Army taking credit for planting that bomb at Blackhawk Security herself. The shooter in the garage, the photos Braxton uncovered. Neither of those were part of the group's MO. "An extremist group bent on protecting Americans' privacy wouldn't run illegal surveillance on their target."

"They didn't seem so concerned about protecting privacy when they threatened to leak officials' browsing histories to the public." Braxton cut her off, his mountainous shoulders blocking her view of the door. "I watch the news, too. These guys have been known to do what it takes to get their message across, violently if forced. The best shot we have to uncovering who's coming after you is Oversight's backdoor access."

The breath she'd been holding rushed from her lungs as the past threatened to overrun the present. She fought back the memories, but how could she when all she thought about when she closed her eyes was the last time she'd accessed that code?

"I told you I can't do that." Her voice rose with each word. He should understand that better than anyone. He'd been there. He'd watched how Oversight's trial run had affected her. No. He didn't get to decide how they handled the threat on her life. He'd lost that right the night he'd walked out on her all those months ago. "This is what we're going to do. First, you're going to get out of my way, so I can review the bomb squad's findings for myself. Second, we're going to arrange to get Vincent the slugs we pulled from the windshield. If he gets a hit on ballistics, you get to keep your end of the deal, and we pretend this whole thing never happened. Go our separate ways."

"I'll keep my end of the deal—" Braxton closed in on her "—but if he doesn't come up with our suspect, I expect you to keep yours."

"Agreed." Silence settled between them. It wasn't an empty silence. It was full of anger, of something else Elizabeth didn't want to identify. "You're pushing me out of the investigation by trying to keep me behind a computer. Why?"

"You know why." Veins fought to burst from beneath his skin. He'd have an embolism if he didn't take a breath. Her guard softened at the concern etched into his features.

"I'm pregnant, Braxton. Not an invalid. I protect my clients, whether it's from behind a desk or strapped in Kevlar, and I'm damn good at my job." Elizabeth shook her head, a disbelieving laugh escaping from between her lips. She tried to swallow around her dry throat. "Just because you're the father of this baby, doesn't give you the right to dictate how I live my…"

Dizziness muddled her vision. She reached out to balance herself, fisting her hand in his T-shirt. She pulled him into her, knees weak. "Whew. If I pass out, don't let it fool you. I'm still going to win this argument when I wake up."

"Liz?" Concern sharpened his voice.

She fought to steady her heart rate. A dull ringing filled her ears as he wrapped his arms around her and led her to the edge of the bed. His clean, masculine scent surrounded her, and she breathed in as much as she could to clear her head. Didn't work. She closed her eyes as the back of her knees hit the mattress. "This conversation is not over."

"Tell me what the hell is happening, or I'm taking you to the hospital right now," he said.

"My blood sugar is low." She'd had it under control the last few days. But running for her life must've forced her body to use up her last meal sooner than she'd expected. She opened her eyes, still clinging to the valleys and ridges of muscle carved into his chest. Nope. Couldn't think about that right now. Food. She needed food. "The baby makes me hypoglycemic. As soon as I eat, I'll be fine."

"Here." Braxton unraveled her fingers from

his shirt but refused to let go of her hand completely as he reached for the bowl on the nightstand. Which actually helped anchor her. Steam still escaped from the glossy red ceramic, and the scent of something spicy and warm filled her as she breathed it in. "This should help."

"What is it?" she said.

"Turkey and vegetable soup." He wiped his palms down his jeans. The mattress dipped with his added weight beside her, and she struggled not to lean into him with everything she had. "The protein should bring your glucose back up in a few minutes. I made more if you need it."

"You made this?" Elizabeth heaved a spoonful into her mouth. Vegetables perfectly cooked, ground turkey flavored with spices. No. Not possible. The Braxton she'd known had survived on a diet of cheap cafeteria food and fast food restaurants. Although, studying the lean muscle across his torso, the new bulges in his arms and thighs, he'd obviously made some changes. Living off junk food didn't carve muscle like that. Her mouth watered for more than the soup in that moment, and she fought to concentrate on not dumping the entire bowl in her lap. The pounding of her heart behind her ears faded. "And look at that, not a gummy worm in sight."

Resting his elbows on his knees, he laughed. "Nope. The only sweets you're going to find in this apartment are chocolate ice cream and rainbow-colored sprinkles."

Elizabeth froze, another spoonful of soup halfway to her mouth. "I still can't believe you remember my favorites."

"How could I forget?" His green-gray gaze, grayer now, centered on her. A smile thinned his mouth, and her grip on the bowl weakened. Damn that smile. Damn the soup. Damn the fact he'd saved her life—twice—in the past three hours. "You kept a pint of ice cream in the freezer at the office and a container of rainbow sprinkles hidden in your desk." Braxton straightened. "I still remember the look on one of the other analysts' face when you screamed at him for five minutes for ignoring the 'do not touch' sign on your ice cream. Bad day for that guy."

"Yeah, well, not all women are made of sugar and spice and everything nice. Some are made of ice cream, rainbow sprinkles and a whole lot of swear words." Elizabeth took another bite, talking around a mouthful of soup, then pointed at him with her spoon. "He was an analyst. He was trained to read between the lines, but he flat out ignored my note. He deserved it. Don't touch my ice cream."

Braxton raised his hands in surrender. "I won't. Not after that."

She couldn't help but laugh. Then caught herself. The man in front of her had done something far worse than ignore a note taped to her ice cream in the office freezer. For the past four months, he'd been the epitome of an uncaring, coldhearted, manipulative jerk who'd taken her to bed then run. But now Braxton refused to fit inside the box she'd created for him in her mind. Elizabeth cleared her throat, more to free her head of his clean scent than anything else, and motioned to him with the empty bowl. "Thanks for the soup. I'm feeling better."

"Anything for you." The sincerity in his voice, the way his hand brushed over her knee closest to him, spiked her flight instinct. Taking the bowl from her, he stood and headed for the door. She couldn't stop the flood of warmth rushing through her. And not just from the soup.

No, no, no. She'd been down this road before. She'd trusted him, relied on him when she'd needed someone the most. He'd been the man who would've done anything to protect her, the man who'd had her back when the NSA sought to destroy her career after Oversight's first real-world test run. But the man in front of her wasn't him. Maybe never had been. And falling for him had left her pregnant and alone.

Wouldn't happen again.

Braxton stopped short of the hallway, as though the weight of her attention cemented his feet in place. His dark hair brushed across his shoulder blades as he rested his head back. "You haven't asked me why I left."

The warmth drained from her system. No. She hadn't.

He turned. The scar cut through his eyebrow shifted as he centered his attention on her. The world threatened to pull out from under her feet when he looked at her like that, like she was the only woman in the world for him.

She glanced over the surveillance photos she'd dropped onto the floor—a dozen Elizabeths staring up at her—but didn't really see the details. "I've spent countless hours obsessing over that question, determined to find out the answer, imagining the moment you'd come back into my life. To be clear, none of it involved a bomb under a conference room table or being shot at in the parking garage."

Locking her attention on Braxton, she tightened her grip on the edge of the mattress. Did he realize how much he'd hurt her? How many nights she'd cried over him leaving? Probably not. Stay in control. Survive the investigation. Move on with her life. That was all she had to do. Elizabeth notched her chin parallel with the floor. "But after finding out I was pregnant a few weeks ago, I decided in the end, I don't care."

All that mattered was that he had, and that he would leave again.

That was the deal.

"I'm sorry. I never meant…" The corners of his mouth turned down, those brilliant eyes filled with…guilt? Braxton shifted his weight between his feet, knuckles white around the bowl in his hand. "I never meant for any of this."

"Fortunately for you, you're not responsible for the man trying to kill me or we'd be having a very different conversation." It was nearly ten at night now. Exhaustion pulled at her muscles, but Elizabeth shoved to her feet. No dizziness. No ringing in her ears. His soup had done its job, and she was about to make sure this baby didn't lower her blood sugar for a few more hours. "Now, take me to the ice cream."

LIZ WAS WRONG. He was responsible. He'd left her unprotected.

Lavender filled his lungs as she maneuvered past him toward the kitchen. His heart rate kicked up a notch. Even after all this time, she affected him in ways he couldn't explain, in ways no other woman had. Only her. "I knew you wouldn't be able to resist."

"Which begs the question, why have it on hand at all?" Liz turned toward him, cocking her head to one side as she shifted her weight against the opposite counter. Still reading between the lines. Back facing the wide expanse of windows and the mesmerizing view, she crossed her arms beneath her chest. Clouds clung to the peaks of the Chugach mountain range, rain hitting the glass in rhythmic intervals, but he only had attention for her. "Unless you knew I'd come back here with you."

There'd been no other option when he'd discovered Oversight's feeds had been hijacked to hunt her down. Not for him. He didn't trust anyone but himself to keep her safe. Braxton wrenched open the freezer door and excavated her favorite brand of chocolate ice cream. "I'm damn good at my job, too."

"True," she said.

"I'm almost afraid you would go with anyone who offered you ice cream and sprinkles, though." He grabbed a bowl and a spoon then scooped two huge servings of ice cream and handed it to her. Holding up one finger, he spun the spice turntable around, pulled rainbow-colored sprinkles from the first tier and offered it to her. "Almost forgot the secret ingredient."

Her fingertips overlapped his for a moment, and something resembling an electric shock shot up his arm. A rush of color climbed up her neck, and he fought the urge to close the small bit of distance between them in the tight galley kitchen. Nice to know he wasn't the only one affected by their proximity.

"You seem to forget the more I weigh, the harder I am to kidnap, so ice cream is essentially saving my life in the long run." Liz dumped an unhealthy amount sprinkles onto her ice cream.

"Good point." A laugh reverberated through him. Although he'd kill anyone who tried. Nobody came after her and survived. The pregnancy only made his protective side stronger. "But I only have enough for the next couple of days, so take it easy."

"If you think we're going to be here for

a couple days, I'll eat it all tonight, and you won't be able to stop me." Liz spooned a heavy bite into her mouth. She closed her eyes, a moan working up her throat. His gut tightened at the sound, all too eager to bring up memories of their one night together. The stress that'd been etched into her features since the moment she'd set sight on him in that damn conference room melted with one spoonful of her favorite dessert.

"Wouldn't dream of it." Anything to make her happy. Even if that included going back into hiding after the investigation ended. His gaze shifted to her lower abdominals, where their daughter barely made herself known in the soft curve there. Even if it meant never meeting his daughter. He would leave to protect them, to make them happy.

Liz opened her eyes, the chocolate brown surrounding her pupils darker than a few minutes ago. The effect raised the hairs on the back of his neck, his entire body on high alert. Because of her. Her rough exhale skimmed across his neck in the small space. "I never thanked you."

"What for?" The edge of the granite countertop cut into his backside, keeping him in the moment. Rain pounded against the windows, a ripple of thunder shaking the framed photos on the walls. He flexed his fingers into the center of his palms. Reminded him of far too many unprotected nights as a kid under that damn fake rock wall in the park when the shelter was full, something he hadn't thought about in years. Until he'd uncovered Liz's new name and address. Of all the places she could've run, she'd chosen Anchorage. To get away from him.

"I wouldn't be standing here if it weren't for you. We wouldn't be standing here." Liz slid her hand over her belly then set her ice cream, only half eaten, on the counter. The sound of stainless steel on ceramic grated in his ears but didn't distract him enough to take his eyes off her. Nothing could. "You saved our lives."

"Which time are you referring to? The bomb, the shootout in the garage or with the bowl of ice cream?" He notched his chin toward her and crossed his boots at the ankles. "I'm losing count."

"All three. Maybe more for the explosion and the shooter than the food, but it certainly helped me from going into hypoglycemic shock." Her brilliant smile rocketed his heart rate into dangerous territory before it disappeared. Gripping the edge of the counter on either side of her waist, Liz locked her gravity-inducing gaze on his, and he felt a pull. "Maybe we can come at this a different way. Forget about the Sovereign Army as a whole for a minute. The shooter in the garage was alone. It was a single-man assault. Looking for one shooter in the group would narrow down our suspect list." She picked up her spoon and bit down against the steel. "Only problem is, if he is a member, I doubt anyone in the Sovereign Army would roll on him."

They'd already been through this.

"I swore I'd keep you alive." Braxton closed the distance between them, her sharp inhale audible as he reached around her for the discarded bowl. Turning his head slightly, he leveled his attention on her right shoulder. Smooth, flawless skin stood out against the black lace of her cap sleeve, and he wanted nothing more than to taste her again, to see if his memory of her was as good as the real thing. He raised his eyes to meet hers. "And I will do anything to keep that promise."

"Protection is not the same thing as controlling someone's life." She swiped her tongue across her lips, pulling his attention to her mouth and the small purple sprinkle stuck to her bottom lip. "If I was meant to be controlled, I would've come with a remote."

"People don't wake up wanting to be victims." His voice came out too rough, too deep. "They don't ask for bad things to happen. They don't ask for pain they have to live with for the rest of their lives. Every day things destroy someone's life. Attacks like today happen. It doesn't matter how strong they are—anyone can get hurt, but I sure as hell won't let it be you and our baby. Understand?"

Sliding one hand along his face, Liz stared at him. Her mouth parted as though the words were on the tip of her tongue. "Braxton—"

His name on her lips was all it took. In one swift move, he threaded his fingers at the nape of her neck and set his forehead against hers. She tried to escape, but the counter kept her caged against him. Damn, he'd missed her. Missed her scent, the way she fit against him perfectly, her sarcasm, the feel of her skin. Electricity lightninged through him as he slid his body in line with hers, her front pressed against him, her hands reaching for his at the back of her neck. Her fingernails bit into the backs of his hands. Hell, no. His memory hadn't done her justice. She breathed against him, her mouth mere centimeters from his. Dropping his hands to her hips, he lifted her onto the counter and centered himself between her thighs. Her fingers fisted in his hair, locking him against her. Right where he needed to be.

What had he been thinking, leaving her behind? He could've told her the truth. Could've asked her to come with him. He moved his fingers back up to her hair, where her erratic pulse beat against the palm of his hand. He did that to her. He changed her breathing patterns. He expanded her pupils so only a thin ring of brown remained. Braxton swallowed hard. Damn it, no. It wouldn't have been fair to expect her to pick up her life and disappear off the radar. Her life was at risk because of him. Because he'd gotten involved with her in the first place. And there was no telling how far that shooter would go to get to her again. Ten minutes ago, nothing would've stopped him from closing that short distance to her mouth, but he couldn't now. He wouldn't put her in danger again.

Spearmint and lavender exploded across his senses, and he reached between them, swiping his thumb across her lip. The sprinkle fell to the kitchen floor, out of sight. He forced himself to cool things down. "You had a purple sprinkle stuck to your mouth."

Liz planted a hand against his chest, his heart fighting for freedom to reach her, and pushed him back. She cleared her throat, the pink in her cheeks and down her neck fading. "It's getting late. I've had a hell of a day. I'm going to go to bed. We can talk about our next step after we've both gotten some rest."

His backside hit the opposite counter. He'd never been more thankful for the granite than in that moment as cold tunneled through his clothing. He nodded and swiped a hand down his face. Lightning streaked through the front windows as the rest of the world came back into focus. "Yeah. Good idea."

She slipped off the counter. Her gaze glittered at him. "Good night, Braxton."

"Good night." Braxton gripped the edge of the counter hard as she headed into the guest bedroom and closed the door behind her. The lock clicked into place, and he nodded as he stared at the tile. Hell, what was he trying to prove? That he still wanted her? No question about it—he'd never stopped wanting her. Never would. But if he'd learned anything over the last four months, it'd been that emotional ties could and would be used against him. Didn't matter what precautions he took or how long he stayed under the radar. Two attempts on her life in the span of an hour was enough for him. There wouldn't be a third.

Chapter Five

She was supposed to be smarter than this.
Stronger.

Muted sunlight filtered around the edges of the thick blackout curtains. They had work to do, but Elizabeth didn't move from the bed. The instant she left this room, reality would set in. Braxton, the shooter, the fact she would most definitely be raising this baby on her own in a few short months. A few more minutes of ignorance. That was all she needed.

Hiking her forearm over her face, she fought to purge the heated moments between her and Braxton from her memory, but her efforts were in vain. The raw desire in his gaze had burned straight through her, marked her. And damn it, she'd almost given in to him. Almost wanted him to kiss her, to make her forget about the fact she'd become a target. A low groan ripped from her throat as she threw the blankets off and hauled herself to her feet.

Ice worked through her veins as she padded barefoot across the cold hardwood floor, hand over her lower abdominals. "We're in trouble, baby girl. And I have no idea how to get us out of it."

She'd survived Braxton leaving once. She wasn't so sure she could do it again.

Get ready and come up with a plan. That was all she had to think about right now. Elizabeth froze, arched over her duffel bag, and cocked her head toward the door. Was that…? No. It couldn't be. Straightening, she headed for the bedroom door and opened it slowly, careful to avoid the creak in the floorboard right outside the guest room. The low *plunk* of guitar strings filtered down the hallway, and she set her head against the door for support, just listening. How long had it been since she'd heard him play? A year? More? The muffled sound of strings from down the hall made it hard to recognize the song but pulled her toward the end all the same.

Before she understood exactly when she'd made the decision to push open his cracked bedroom door, there he was. Her insides constricted at the wide expanse of ridges and valleys of muscle flexing across his back as he played, his hair brought back in a loose ponytail to keep it out of his way. Despite the release and contraction of muscles in his broad shoulders, he looked completely at ease, relaxed. And hell if that didn't vault her heart into her throat.

"Did I wake you?" His voice barely registered over the low chord of music, only one side of his features visible from her position at the door.

"No, I can blame that on your daughter at all hours of the night." She shifted her weight into the door frame and crossed her arms. He kept playing, kept pulling at some part of her she thought she'd buried for good when he'd left. The same part that had protected her against wondering where he'd gone, who he'd been with, if he'd ever had feelings for her. "I wasn't sure you'd kept it. When I searched your apartment after…" Elizabeth dropped her attention to his discarded shirt at the edge of the bed and centered her focus. No point in rehashing the past. Wouldn't change anything. "Everything was still there."

Except the guitar she'd bought for him for his birthday last year, the one he held now. That alone had clued her in that something hadn't happened to him. He'd left.

"You are the only person who's ever given me a birthday present. Did I ever tell you that? We never had a lot of money growing up, but after my dad lost his job, then the house, we had nothing. My mom tried. Collected aluminum can tops for me—one for every year—and strung them on a necklace my dad had given her when they were dating. But this…" Braxton paused, sliding his fingers up the guitar's neck, across the engraving she'd had done in the guitar shop. *Everything is better with sprinkles.* They were supposed to be best friends forever. Her fingernails dug into her arm, keeping her in the moment. He finally locked those brilliant green eyes on her as he rocked forward on the edge of the mattress, and a rush of heat flooded through her. "Do you remember the chords I taught you?"

A burst of laughter escaped from between her lips as she shook her head. He'd spent hours trying to teach her to play. Didn't work. She was the least musically inclined person in existence. "Not a single one."

Braxton shifted on the mattress, making room at the end. With a single nod, he beckoned her forward. "Come here."

Her lungs seized, but the rest of her body refused to follow her brain's orders to fight. They needed to come up with another plan to identify the man trying to kill her. Not mess around on his guitar. Still, she put one foot in front of the other until the backs of her knees hit the mattress, and she sat down beside him. Warmth flooded down her left side as his arm brushed against hers.

Braxton set the instrument across her lap, one hand wrapped around the neck, the other sliding between her arm and her rib cage. A shiver chased down her spine despite the fact she was burning up inside. Goose bumps pimpled down her arms as he set his mouth close to her ear. And the world disintegrated from in front of her, leaving only the two of them and his guitar. He fit his fingers over hers, the calluses rough against her, as she settled against him. Flashing her that gut-wrenching smile, he studied her face from forehead to chin as he forced her fingers to move with his. "You got it."

"It sounds like I'm skinning a cat." His laugh reverberated down her side, and Elizabeth tightened her grip on the guitar. She stilled, heart threatening to beat out of her chest, as she turned her head toward him. She rolled her lips between her teeth. His gaze shot to her mouth as the thick ring of green around his pupils disappeared.

One breath. Two.

"You're doing great." He strengthened his hold on her, almost pressing her into him as he had the night before. He felt so good right now. Her head begged her to run, to not go down this path again, but her body had taken control the second she'd walked into that conference room. After the explosion, the shooter in the garage, she needed this. Needed him.

The shrill ring of her burner phone from the other room brought her back to reality.

She blinked, shook her head. Shifting forward, away from him, she cleared her throat and ran a hand through her hair. Wow. What the hell had she been thinking? Elizabeth shoved to her feet. "That's Vincent. I gave him the number in case he made progress in the investigation."

Setting the guitar up against the wall, Braxton reached for his discarded long-sleeve shirt. "Better answer it then."

She nodded, escaping down the hallway. The problem was she hadn't been thinking. That'd always been the problem when he was around. She shook off the rush of comfort that'd settled into her bones and hurried to answer the phone. "Vincent, hey—"

"Elizabeth Bosch," an unfamiliar voice said. "Or should I call you Elizabeth Dawson now? Remind me, which one of you created Oversight and single-handedly destroyed over a thousand people's lives with one press of a button?"

Her blood froze in her veins. She hit the speaker feature on the screen and dropped the phone away from her ear. Hitting the home button, she raced to record the call and took a deep breath to steady her nerves. "How did you get this number?"

"You're not the only one who can run a trace. I've got my sources, too." Static reached through the line, making it hard to identify any kind of background noise. But the man from the garage—maybe the same one who tried blowing her up—was a professional. If that same man was on the other side of the line, he'd thought this through, made contingencies. There wouldn't be any mistakes on his end. "I almost had you back at Blackhawk Security. I would have, too, if it hadn't been for your new bodyguard. Have to admit, I hadn't accounted for him."

Confirmation. They were dealing with a professional.

A tingling sensation climbed up her spine, and she turned.

Braxton stood in the doorway, rage and violence carved into his features.

"You set the bomb in the conference room. You knew I had a meeting in there and timed it just right." She needed confirmation, needed to know they were looking for a single suspect in a numberless group of possibilities. She tipped the phone's microphone closer to her mouth and forced herself to focus on the caller, the man who had tried twice now to kill her. "Well, not perfectly. I was halfway out the door when you triggered the explosion. So you had to make sure your target wouldn't get away. That's why you came after me in the garage."

"I'm not going to let you get away with what you've done." Heavy breathing interrupted the static through the line.

Elizabeth swallowed around the dryness in her throat. "What do you want from me?"

"I want you at Town Square Park in one hour. Alone," he said.

Glancing up at Braxton, she licked her lips. The man she'd known—the man she'd loved—had disappeared in the span of a few seconds. All from an unknown voice on the other line. Tension tightened the muscles down her spine as she considered the situation. "And if I don't show?"

"I know who you've been spending your nights with, Elizabeth. I know why your grocery bill has nearly doubled the past few months, why you visit the park so often after work." Another flicker of static from the other line, then muffled words. Then the undeniable sound of a bullet loading into a gun chamber. "Would you really want him caught up in the middle of this?"

No. No, no, no, no. Elizabeth straightened a bit despite the urge to collapse back on to the bed nearly consuming her. "He has nothing to do with any of this."

"One hour," the shooter said. "I'll be waiting."

The call ended.

She stared at the phone. Either she walked straight into what was undoubtedly a trap or she risked losing the only family her daughter might have left once Braxton disappeared.

"Who have you been spending your nights with, Liz?" She almost didn't recognize Braxton's voice. Too distant. Too dangerous. Her stomach flipped at the sight of the violence still burned into his expression, in the tightness of all those new muscles. "Who was he talking about?"

"Okay. I was going to tell you earlier, but the timing never seemed right." She tossed the phone onto the bed. Braxton wouldn't hurt her. Never her. But the thought of telling him the truth dried her mouth. A wave of nausea threatened to unbalance her, but whether it was from the possibility of revealing what she'd been doing in her spare time or morning sickness, she had no idea. Elizabeth straightened. He deserved to know. No matter how hard the truth would be to get out or how much he'd hate her afterward. "Since I moved to Anchorage, I've been looking after your father."

HIS LUNGS PROTESTED as though he'd been hit in the chest with a two-by-four. She what? "That man literally put us out on the street when I was a kid to support his habit, and you've been visiting him? Bringing him food?"

"He's not the man you remember, Braxton. The drugs..." Liz took a step closer, but where her proximity usually relieved the pressure coursing through him, it now made it stronger. She seemed to realize her effect on him and froze, that full bottom lip dropping open. "Sometimes he recognizes me, asks about you, asks about the baby. Most of the time I'm the only person keeping him alive."

Was that supposed to make him feel better? She'd never met his father when they'd worked together at Fort Meade. Which meant she'd come to Anchorage and tracked the old man down. She'd spent night after night making sure he had a roof over his head when the addict hadn't even had the guts to do the same for his own flesh and blood.

"And now whoever is coming after you is using him as leverage."

"I'm sorry," she said. "I didn't know the shooter was watching me—"

"Why?" His head spun. His vision was a blur, a haze of everything but the woman in front of him. A woman who'd betrayed his deepest secret. The old man he'd called Dad for years had never chosen his family over the poison he could buy on the street. Never even bothered to show up to his mother's funeral after she'd caught a cold and died from pneumonia lying in a cardboard box. Because of his father. Because of what he did to their family. Braxton had grown up without the support he'd needed at the time, and he'd vowed never to fall back into that old man's manipulations again. The SOB was selfish. Only looking for a way to score. "I told you about what that man put me and my mother through, what happened to her. Why would you look for him? Why would you try to help him?"

"You weren't here, Braxton. You left." Her lips thinned as she rolled them between her teeth. "And this baby deserves a family."

His blood pressure spiked. Of course she deserved a family. Every baby did. Someone to sing to her at night, to kiss her in the morning, to help her count her fingers and toes. "You don't need him. I can give her that. I'm her father."

"For how long?" she asked.

"What?" What the hell did that mean? She'd told him he was the father.

"How long are you going to be around?" Liz pulled back her shoulders. The oversize T-shirt and baggy sweatpants did nothing to hide her mouthwatering curves underneath as she interlaced her fingers under her lower abdominals. "The NSA interrogated me after your disappearance. They claimed you sold classified intel to an anonymous third party. They're not going to stop looking for you until they've got you in cuffs. So how long are you going to stick around before you choose to go back into hiding?"

He didn't have an answer. The idea of being a distant father—having practically grown up with a shell of one himself—was too much. He couldn't do that to his daughter. And no way would he do that to Liz. Anxiety wound itself through his gut. But serving a possible life sentence behind bars for treason wouldn't do them a damn bit of good, either.

"As much as you might hate that man, he's still your father. He has a lot to answer for, but right now, he needs our help. And I'm going to give it to him." She nodded, her expression resigned, as she strode past him toward the bedroom door. "Now if you'll excuse me, I need to find a hammer to smash this phone to pieces before it gives up anything else today."

He couldn't fight the smile pulling at his mouth as he envisioned her with a hammer in one hand and her burner phone in the other. The shooter shouldn't have been able to get a lock on that number so easily. Braxton had checked that phone personally, along with the others in his stash. No spyware. They were new numbers, too. Which meant her Blackhawk Security teammate Vincent Kalani, the only person to reach Liz at that number, could've been compromised and not even know it. Or if he did... What had he read in the ex-cop's file? Something about taking bribes. The forensics expert had some explaining to do. He called back over his shoulder but didn't follow Liz from the room. "Check under the kitchen sink."

Hell, he couldn't face her yet. Disbelief still coursed through him as he studied the personal belongings she'd left in plain sight from her duffel bag. She'd been taking care of his father these last few months. Every night. And now his old man was being used as leverage against her, and Braxton was expected to risk

Liz's life for a man who'd done nothing but disappoint him for years. The meeting was a trap. If he lost her…

No. It wouldn't happen. Without her, there would be no one else. And that wasn't an option. He'd already lost too many people in his life. He wasn't about to lose her, too.

Heavy thumps echoed down the hall, and he worked to shove his own selfish need to keep her in his life to the back of his mind. Sounded like Liz had found the hammer. He spun toward the door to survey the damage but froze as the edge of a photo stuffed into her duffel bag claimed his attention. Not a photo. A black-and-white sonogram. Checking back over his shoulder as another round of hammering reached his ears, he closed in on the bag. His hand shook as he reached for the single piece of thin, glossy paper. Liz's name, the date of the sonogram, the doctor's office and the measurements in centimeters stood out in white lettering around the edge of the dark background. But there, right in the center of the cone-shaped ultrasound, was a baby.

His baby. Sixteen weeks old.

Her perfectly shaped head, her knees drawn up almost to her nose. Braxton couldn't make out much else, but he didn't have to. She was perfect. Sliding his thumb over where he thought her right ear might be, he exhaled hard at a block of letters he hadn't seen before. His heart dropped.

Baby Karina.

Liz had named their daughter after his mother.

He rubbed his free hand over his face and turned toward the door. Five steps. That was all it took before she came into sight. He couldn't breathe—couldn't think—as he closed in on her. Catching her wrist before she swung the hammer down into the debris of what used to be a cell phone, he twisted her into him.

Her eyes widened. "Braxton, what—"

He crushed his mouth against hers. Fire burned through him, raising the hairs on the back of his neck. Sliding one hand around her back, he fought to bring her closer, make her a permanent part of himself. The scent of lavender worked through him, filled him as her pulse beat hard in her wrist beneath his fingertips. Forget the explosion. Forget the shooter. Forget the charges he'd face once the NSA realized he'd stayed in the country. Braxton only had attention for this moment. Only had Liz.

And she kissed him back.

Her grip loosened around the hammer

and it fell, barely missing her bare feet. He released his grip on her wrist then held his breath as she planted her palms against his chest. But not to shove him away. Her lips, soft and silky, pressed into his. He licked the edge of her bottom lip then drew it between his teeth.

A gasp escaped her control, and his blood pressure skyrocketed. He thrust his tongue into her mouth, every cell in his body determined to make her his. He set the sonogram on the counter behind her then threaded his fingers into her hair at the base of her skull in a tight grip. Exploring, memorizing, claiming, he consumed her as a dehydrated man consumed water. Damn, she tasted good. How had he been able to live without her all this time? How had he been able to walk away?

Desire blazed inside him as he kicked the hammer out of the way and maneuvered her toward the same countertop he'd caged her against last night. He felt too rough for her, too punishing, but he couldn't stop. Not until he'd claimed every inch or she told him to back off. She tasted too good, and he'd become addicted to that taste a long time ago. What he wouldn't give to kiss her senseless every morning.

The calluses on his fingertips caught against smooth skin along her midsection.

Hell.

Braxton pulled away then set his forehead against hers. His lungs fought to catch up with his racing pulse. As much as he wanted to strip her bare and help her forget the past two days, he couldn't…they couldn't. They'd run out of time. "The meeting."

He couldn't say much else. Not when she was still pressed against him, when her touch seared him down to his core.

"Right. Shooter. Trap." Her short exhales beat against the underside of his jaw, those brown eyes swirling with confused desire. She blinked then dropped her hands away from him. "I need to change out of my sweats. My shoulder holster doesn't exactly work with this shirt."

"You look good in anything you put on." A laugh rumbled from deep in his chest. His fingertips grazed over the bare column of her throat before he put a good amount of space between them. He had to. Otherwise, they might never leave the safe house. Notching her chin higher, he forced her to meet his gaze. "I won't let him touch you, Sprinkles."

She nodded. "I know."

"Good." He needed her to believe him. "Then let's catch us a bomber."

Chapter Six

When he'd kissed her, she'd lost all restraint.

One second, she'd been working out her frustration at putting an innocent man in danger, at not being able to hold up her emotional guard against Braxton, on the burner phone, and the next his mouth had been on hers. Her heart had thundered so hard, blood pouring through her ears, she'd felt as though she'd been underwater. Couldn't breathe. Couldn't hear. But she hadn't been able to pull away.

Pushing the memory back—a memory she'd never let go—Elizabeth cracked her knuckles as she walked east down the sidewalk toward the Alaska Center for the Performing Arts. She stuffed her shaking hands into her now empty coat pockets and hunkered deeper into the faux-fur folds as a blast of frigid air fought to chase the heat from her skin. They'd handed off the bullets from the SUV's windshield to Vincent as soon as they'd arrived, but she doubted he'd be able to glean anything useful. Whoever had tried to kill her had been planning this from the beginning. He wouldn't slip up unless he meant to slip up. She scanned the rooftops of the surrounding buildings. And the chances of that seemed slight. "No sign of our target yet."

Anchorage's snow-covered Town Center stretched a half acre in front of her. Blue and white Christmas lights had yet to be removed from the branches of pines decorating the grounds, even though the holiday season had ended three weeks ago. Her boots fought for purchase on the icy sidewalk. Or was it the possibility she might be centered in a shooter's crosshairs unbalancing her? Cloud cover made it hard to see into the shadows, and the hairs on the back of her neck stood on end.

"He'll show. You're too good of an opportunity to pass up." Braxton's voice in her ear settled the rush of nervous energy shooting down her spine. Well, that, and the fact he'd taken position thirty yards to her right in case he had to get to her fast. Mostly settled her nerves. There was still the issue of a possible ambush, and the conversation they would have to have after this little operation was over. About him leaving again. The open line between their earpieces crackled as the wind kicked up. A haze of snow danced in front of her. "Remember, I've got a giant bowl of ice cream and rainbow sprinkles waiting for you when this is over. So you better make it out of this alive."

"You always know exactly what to say." Studying the park for a second time, she fought the urge to look in Braxton's direction. The caller had told her to come alone. He should've tried convincing her bodyguard. She slowed her progress as she approached a single snow-covered bench in the middle of the park. With January temperatures dropping by the minute, most visitors had gone inside to warm up. Lower risk of putting innocent bystanders in danger if things went south.

"The cavalry has arrived, and guess what? I brought the big guns." Elliot Dunham's voice penetrated through the stiffness gripping her shoulders and neck, and a smile automatically stretched across her lips. What would they do without Blackhawk Security's con man turned private investigator? Rescued by the CEO and founder of the security firm from an Iraqi prison on fraud charges, the reformed criminal with a genius-level IQ never failed to amuse her. No matter how many times his compulsive sarcasm grated on her nerves, he'd never failed to have her back in the three months they'd worked together. And she'd always have his. "Admit it, Dawson, you missed me."

Gratitude flooded through her. Calling in Blackhawk Security had been her idea, but Braxton had taken point in getting them in place. She buried her mouth in the lining of her coat to hide her response in case the shooter had already arrived and was searching for signs she hadn't come alone. "If by big guns you mean Vincent and Glennon, then yes, I missed you."

"They won't let me touch the sniper rifle without taking a class first." Elliot's lighthearted attitude and the additional backup helped alleviate the nausea building in her stomach. Short exhales said he was still trying to get in position. "Personally, I think they like being the only ones with the heavy-duty weapons."

"Does this guy ever shut up?" Braxton asked.

"No." Vincent Kalani entered the park to her left, head down, barely raising his attention to her before he cut across the open terrain. Hands stuffed into his coat pockets, he moved with lethal grace. The former cop hid his face beneath a mane of wavy dark hair, but the tattoos climbing up his neck stood out. If the shooter had done his research, there was a good chance he'd recognize Blackhawk's forensics expert. "Trust me, we've tried."

"Head in the game, gentlemen." Glennon Chase, the firm's newest recruit and recent wife to their weapons expert, slid into sight at the edge of Elizabeth's peripheral vision. Armed with her own rifle, the former army investigator nodded as Elizabeth took a seat on the bench. Planting her eye against her scope, Glennon shifted out of sight along the rooftop of the building overlooking the park. "I've got movement at the north end of the park."

Elizabeth fought against the urge to look. Instead, she surveyed the area as a whole before redirecting her attention to the man stumbling toward her. Stained jacket, ripped jeans, thick gray hair and beard. Recognition flared, and she pushed off the bench. Wild eyes locked on her as Brolin Levitt reached for her, a prominent limp in his left leg. "Don't shoot. He's not the target." Slowing her approach, she lifted her hands, palms facing him. "Brolin, it's me. Elizabeth. You remember me? I'm friends with your son, Braxton."

Same introduction. Same approach. Every time. Over the past few months, the chances of him recognizing her steered toward sixty-forty. Sixty percent of the time, he didn't remember his own name. He closed in on her faster than she thought possible for a drug-addled old man.

Brolin didn't answer.

"Liz, I've got a bad feeling about this." Braxton's concern echoed through the ear-piece, but she didn't pay it any attention. He'd made his feelings for his father perfectly clear, and there wasn't any scenario in which he'd trust the man in front of her. She didn't care. Brolin was innocent in all of this and had obviously been injured.

"I'm wearing Kevlar, I've got a gun and I know how to use it," she said. "I'm only helpless when my nail polish is wet, and even then, I can pull a trigger if I have to."

"While you make valid points, the shooter drew you here using Brolin as leverage. So why let the old man go?" he asked.

"I think I know why." Elizabeth caught a glimpse of two wires coming from the bottom of Brolin's stained old jacket. Her breath caught in her throat. Every cell in her body froze. One second. Two. Too long. "Braxton, your father is wired."

"What?" he asked.

A gunshot echoed off the surrounding buildings.

She spun toward the sound.

Braxton broke away from his position at her left, his ball cap flying off his head as he pumped his arms and legs hard. "Liz, get down!"

Pain splintered across her left arm and she spun, clamping her hand over the graze. She hit the ground hard. Snow and ice worked through her clothing as she scrambled toward Brolin. The shooter had used Brolin and the bomb strapped to his chest as a distraction. Long enough to get her in his sights. Fisting her hands around his jacket, Elizabeth wrenched the old man into her and pushed him forward. Her boots slid against the dusting of snow covering the sidewalks. They had to get moving. They were still out in the open. "Find that damned shooter."

"Got him. Suspect is rabbiting across the roof of the building to the south. There's a car waiting in the alley between buildings. Alaska license plate echo, uniform, sierra, six, eight, seven." Vincent's calm did nothing to ease the adrenaline surging through her veins. "Can't get a clean shot. Glennon?"

Braxton wrapped his hand around her arm and hauled her and Brolin their feet. He shoved them ahead of him as a black GMC pulled up to the curb fifty feet away.

The front passenger window lowered, revealing Elliot Dunham's dumbass smirk. "This never would've happened if they let me have a sniper rifle."

"Now's not the time, Elliot!" They reached the SUV. Elizabeth wrenched the passenger side door open and threw Brolin inside. No time for hellos. There was a shooter on the loose. "Meet your new assignment. His name is Brolin Levitt. He dies, you die. Understand?"

Elliot's deep gray eyes widened. "Is that a bomb?"

"I'm pretty sure it's fake, but you might want to take a look at it just in case." She slammed the door closed, not waiting for an answer.

"I've got a shot." The familiar sound of Glennon loading a round into the rifle's chamber echoed in Elizabeth's earpiece as Braxton forced her to take cover behind a park bench. The SUV fishtailed away from the curb, shooting down the street. Brolin was safe. "I'm taking it."

The thunderclap of another bullet leaving the barrel of a rifle thudded through her. She held her breath as Braxton wrapped her in a tight hold against his chest. Waited. Silence settled around her. Her pulse throbbed at the base of her throat, the pain in her arm pulling at her attention. The second shot hadn't been meant for her, but a rush of relief escaped from her lungs all the same. Sirens filtered through the pulsing in her head.

"I missed him." Glennon hauled her rifle off the edge of the rooftop above and disappeared from sight. "If anybody tells my husband I missed that shot, you're dead."

"How are you going to kill us when you can't even hit your target?" The growl of the SUV's engine filtered through Elliot's earpiece. Good. Brolin would be safe as long as he stuck with Blackhawk's private investigator. Although getting him to stay might be a challenge, but she was sure Elliot would figure something out.

"I'm starting with you, Elliot," Glennon said.

Squealing tires reached her ears as Elizabeth caught sight of a high-class Mercedes sedan fishtailing out of the alley across the street. The windows were too tinted for her to make an identification, but her instincts said that was their shooter. She dug her nails into Braxton's jacket. "He's getting away."

"No, he's not." Braxton wrapped his hand around hers, tugging her after him. "You remember that license plate number?"

"Yes." Puffs of her breath crystallized in

front of her, freezing air reaching down to the bullet graze on her arm through the new hole in her jacket. The pain slid to the back of her mind as she forced her legs to work harder.

"Good." Braxton pulled her around the south corner of the park, toward another Blackhawk Security SUV. "Get in."

HE WASN'T GOING to let Liz become a victim from circumstances he'd created. If he hadn't tried to keep her in the dark in the first place, she wouldn't be in this situation. And if that bullet hadn't only grazed her arm, he'd have had to live with that the rest of his life. The idea pushed his foot against the accelerator harder. Everyone was created by a defining event. Something that changed them just enough. A loss, a trauma, the end of a relationship. Liz would be his. Always his. "You okay?"

"I'm fine. Focus on the road." She clamped a hand over the wound in her arm, swaying as he forced the SUV around a tight turn. Downtown Anchorage blurred in his peripheral vision as they closed in on the Mercedes's bumper. A minivan pulled out in front of them, and he swerved. She grabbed onto the handle above her head with one hand and the dashboard with the other with a groan of pain. "If I ever need a skilled getaway driver, you are not the person I'm going to call."

Uneven roads lifted them out of their seats. The shooter barreled through a construction zone ahead of them, taking a sharp right.

Liz tapped her earpiece with bloody fingertips. "Vincent, we need Anchorage PD to set up a roadblock. We can't let this guy get away."

"Copy that," Vincent said.

"Hang on." Braxton made the turn, the SUV's fender barely missing a car pulling out of an underground parking garage. Checking back over his shoulder, he shook his head. "Don't people know how to drive anymore?"

Liz swiped her hand across her face, attention out the windshield. "For crying out loud, it's not this psychopath who's going to kill me. It's your driving."

Those words hit him like a hammer fall. Braxton sobered, knuckles tight around the steering wheel as they cleared downtown, and sped up the ramp onto south Seward Highway. If the bastard thought he'd be able to lose them by disappearing into the trail entrances along the coast, he was wrong. Braxton had had to know them better than anyone else in this city in order to survive on his own. "I'm not going to let anything happen to you."

"You guys realize your coms are still on-line, right?" Elliot's voice in his head was not what he needed right now. "This seems like a private moment."

"All you need to worry about is keeping Brolin alive, Elliot. Leave the rest to me." Liz shot a quick look in his direction. While putting his old man under Blackhawk Security protection hadn't climbed its way to the top of Braxton's priority list, the drug addict could at least do some good to identify the shooter who'd taken him. "Vincent, we've turned south onto Seward Highway, and this guy isn't showing any signs of stopping. Where are we at with Anchorage PD?"

"There's a pileup downtown, thanks to your driver there." Vincent's disappointment echoed through the earpiece. "And any other available units are closing in on the park due to a wave of calls about shots fired. I'm having the chief send as many as he can your way, but that could be up to an hour."

Braxton picked the device out of his ear and tossed it into the back seat, eyes on the prize ahead. He maneuvered around a fifty-two-foot semitruck, losing sight of the Mercedes for three seconds. Four. Cloud cover made it that much harder to keep their target straight, but he soon had a lock on the shooter again. The bastard wasn't going to get away. Not when they were so close to ending this nightmare. Desperation clawed up his throat. He'd vowed to protect the woman in the seat beside him. He couldn't let her down now. "Guess we're on our own."

"You want to be the one to catch him." Her voice worked to ease the tangle of tension coiling tight at the base of his skull. The Mercedes swerved to maneuver around a group of three cars ahead, but she'd always been able to consume his attention with a single look. A word. "Why?"

The engine growled in protest as he pushed the SUV harder, trying to close the distance between them and the shooter. He had no idea what they were going to do after that, but he'd always been good on his feet. The sun would start going down in the next hour. They'd lose him altogether if they didn't end this.

"You know why. I told you I'd protect you, and I meant it. Catching this guy is the only way to do that." He locked his jaw against the lie, the muscles along his neck and shoulders straining. Chancing a quick glance at her, he read the questions carved into her expression.

"No, that's not it. It's something more than that." The weight of her attention pinned him to the back of the leather seat. She'd never been an analyst, but she could make a damn good career out of reading people. How the hell did he think he could keep secrets from her? "What aren't you telling me?"

The Mercedes disappeared in the midst of four cars ahead of them.

Braxton sat forward in his seat as he sped around a small sedan. Narrowing his gaze, he studied car after car as he backed his foot off the accelerator. "He's gone."

"What?" She turned her attention back to the road then twisted in her seat to inspect the cars behind them. "That's not possible. There aren't any exit ramps in this section of the highway."

Didn't make the shooter's disappearing act any less real. Braxton checked his rearview mirror as a pair of headlights flared to life behind them. "He didn't get off the highway. Get ready—"

Two gunshots broke the soothing sound of tires against asphalt, but the bullets ricocheted off the glass. Bulletproof windows were a nice touch. Braxton swerved into the next lane, narrowly avoiding another sedan, but the maneuver did nothing to distract the shooter. The hood of the Mercedes closed in fast.

"He's going to try to run us off the road." Panic tinted Liz's words, but he couldn't worry about that right now. Keeping her alive. That was all that mattered. She could panic all she wanted as long as she was alive.

The first hit to the bumper thrust them forward. The steering wheel jerked in his hand, but Braxton kept a tight hold. Civilian cars slowly backed off as another collision to their bumper forced them onto the highway's shoulder. The grooves cut into the shoulder to keep drivers awake drowned out another gunshot to the back of the SUV. He fought to keep the SUV on the road, but slowing down, pulling over even, would put Liz directly in the shooter's sights. Not an option. Time to end this, but with the Turnagain Arm waterway on one side and nothing but thick wilderness on the other, he only had a small window to make this work. "Hang on to something."

Her hand shot to the handlebar above her head just before Braxton slammed on the brakes. Tires screeched in his ears, the smell of burned rubber filling the interior of the SUV as momentum thrust them forward in their seats. The Mercedes's headlights disappeared behind the bottom of the back window. His lungs seized half a second before the shooter rammed into the back of their vehicle. The third collision forced the SUV to one side despite how hard Braxton pulled the wheel in the opposite direction.

Tires caught on the road. The world went hazy as the vehicle wrenched to one side then flipped. Every instinct he owned urged him to reach out for Liz. He loosened his grip on the steering wheel, fighting against gravity to touch her, but the highway rushed up to meet the windshield too fast. The terrorizing fear etched into her features vanished as the roof crumpled under the impact. His head snapped forward, glass breaking all around them. Metal protested against asphalt in his ears, but all he could focus on was Liz's scream.

The SUV swung up again, depleting his brain of oxygen, then slammed into the ground. The seat belt cut into his shoulder and across his chest.

Then there was stillness as the vehicle righted itself.

His head throbbed in rhythm to his racing heartbeat. A dull ringing filled his ears, but not loud enough to block out the screech of tires nearby. He blinked against the onslaught of chaos surrounding the SUV, vision hazy, tongue thick in his mouth. "Liz."

No answer.

Braxton strained to look at her. "Liz, baby, can you hear me?"

Footsteps heightened the headache spreading from the crown of his head. Something wet—blood—trickled down the side of his face. He'd hit his head against the driver's side window during the roll. Shadows crossed his vision on Liz's side of the vehicle. Wait, no. Just one. The outline of a man closed in on the SUV.

Black ski mask. Pressed suit. Gun in his hand. Every muscle in his body tensed. Not a civilian.

"Come on, Sprinkles, wake up." The seat belt kept Braxton secured in the seat. He fought to reach for his gun that'd fallen from his shoulder holster. He couldn't move his arms, stomach rocketing into his throat. He leveraged his heels into the floorboards but couldn't move otherwise. "Elizabeth!"

The shooter reached in through the broken passenger side window—too close to Liz— and unlocked the door. Raising the gun in his hand toward Braxton, he wrenched the door open then reached for Liz's seat belt. The SOB wasn't going to take her. Not happening. Dark eyes centered on him. "Well, that went easier than I imagined."

Braxton didn't recognize the voice, the posture, the suit. No accent. Nothing to lead him to an identity of the man taking the most important thing in his life from him.

"I'm going to kill you, you bastard." Braxton ordered his body to move, to reach for his gun, to do anything. No response. A feral scream ripped from his throat. Blood and sweat stung his eyes. He couldn't lose her. Not yet. Not when she'd just come back into his life. "I'm going to hunt you down, and I'm going to end you."

The shooter laughed, dark, merciless, as he compressed the button to Liz's seat belt, wrapped his grip around her delicate wrist and hefted her over one shoulder. All the while keeping the gun aimed on Braxton. "Good luck with that."

Chapter Seven

Pain. Dizziness. A hard pulsing behind her ears that she could only describe as the beginning of her own death.

She felt as though she'd been weighed down by lead. Elizabeth struggled to open her eyes, blinking back the heaviness in her brain. Blackness consumed the edges of her vision. She narrowed in on the movement of patterns in front of her. Blackness and... pinstripes? The subtle lines shifted, and she realized the unbalanced sensation charging through her wasn't dizziness, but movement. The intense pressure in her midsection meant someone had flipped her over their shoulder and was carrying her. She used her remaining strength to raise her head. Tendrils of hair blocked her peripheral vision, but there, straight behind her, was the remains of her destroyed SUV. Sullivan wasn't going to be too happy about another of Blackhawk Security's vehicles being totaled, but she couldn't afford to care. Not with a shooter on their tail. Wait. Confusion gripped her in a tight vise as she sank back against the man carrying her. "Braxton?"

"Not exactly." That voice. She recognized that voice from somewhere.

A whiff of expensive cologne tickled her nose and worked deep into her lungs. No. Not Braxton. He didn't wear cologne. Which meant... Recognition clicked into place. The air rushed from her lungs. The shooter. He'd called her on the burner phone. He'd—

A thread of anxiety unraveled inside her, tangling up with anger, resentment and fear. The edge of her shoulder holster dug into her armpit, but with one look, she discovered she'd been relieved of her weapon. Black asphalt passed beneath her. *Think, think, think.* Rolling her hands into fists, Elizabeth focused all of her attention on the small of the shooter's back and sank her elbow hard in the curve of his spine as hard as she could.

His grip around the back of her knees disappeared, and she toppled backward. The highway rushed up to meet her faster than she expected, and she hit the ground. Loose rocks cut into the side of her head, but she rolled in an effort to get to her feet. Stinging pain spread across the other side of her skull as the shooter fisted a chunk of her hair in his hand and hauled her to her feet.

Six-foot-plus frame, lean, preferred a Windsor knot and a nice suit over Kevlar. It wasn't much to go on, but it was a start. Elizabeth wrapped her grip around his wrist as he wrenched her into him. The black ski mask hid his mouth as he spoke, but those dark eyes would always stick in her memory. Cold. Calculating. Dangerous. "You're going to pay for that, but first, you're going to help me."

"You've tried to kill me three times and put an innocent man's life in danger." Her voice remained steady despite the earthquake exploding inside her. "There's no way I'd do anything to help you."

"We'll see about that." Pulling his weapon, the shooter wrenched her into his side and aimed for the totaled SUV. For Braxton still in the driver's seat. "You should've known changing your last name wouldn't stop me from finding you, Elizabeth. Not when I have Oversight at my disposal." He pressed his mouth against her ear, and a shiver threatened to overrun her. "How about now? Should I pull this trigger, or are you going to get in the damn car?"

Bystanders' screams and panic infiltrated

through the pounding of her pulse in her ears. Car doors slammed; tires peeled against the road. Others raised their phones to get the scene on video or capture a photo but didn't move to interfere. She couldn't breathe. Couldn't think.

Braxton's life or her own certain death.

"Liz, run!" His voice punctured through the sensory overload wrapping itself in a tight fist inside. Braxton struggled to free himself from the crumpled SUV, pulling against the seat belt. The sound of liquid hitting the road claimed her attention. She scanned the wreckage until sunlight reflected off a pool of gas beneath the SUV. Any second now the vehicle could catch fire, and Braxton would be gone.

"If you kill him now, you lose your leverage. I'll never help you." Her heart turned over in her chest, her stomach squeezing tight. No. She wasn't going to leave him. He wouldn't leave her. With the shooter's forearm braced against her collarbones, there was only one thing she could do.

"True, but you've made yourself a new life here. Gotten to know quite a few people." His laugh rumbled between her shoulder blades. "I have an entire list of leverage, Elizabeth. And I'm not above ticking them off one at a time until you do as I ask. Elliot Dunham,

Vincent Kalani, Sullivan Bishop. And your friend Kate? Hasn't she lost enough?" He moved his finger over the trigger, cocking his head away from her neck. "But today, I think I'll start with your bodyguard there."

She locked her attention on Braxton. "Come find me when this is over."

"Good girl." The shooter dropped his weapon to his side. "Now get in the car."

"No." She took advantage. Inhaling deeply, Elizabeth dropped to her haunches. She rocked back on her heels and sprang back up, shoving her shoulder into his midsection to knock him off balance. He hit the ground, the gun sliding across the asphalt. They both followed its track. One second, two, and then Elizabeth lunged. The shooter recovered almost instantly. Any physical fight could cost her everything, but she wasn't going to let him hurt anyone else. Not when she could end this now. Her best option was that gun. She wrapped her fingers around the barrel as a shoe stomped on her wrist. Bone crunched, and a scream worked up her throat.

"Elizabeth!" Braxton's yell barely registered over the high-pitched ringing in her ears.

The shooter bent down to claim the weapon from her. "You're not going to win, Elizabeth. I've been waiting for this moment for too long. You're going to help me. Even if I have to kill everyone you've ever cared about to force your compliance."

She hadn't been trained in combat like Blackhawk's weapons expert Anthony Harris, hadn't been trained to fight like a SEAL as Sullivan had. Hell, even Glennon could take down a room full of men on her own if pushed. But Elizabeth wouldn't give up. Her life wasn't the only one that mattered anymore. She was this baby's mother, and she would do everything in her power to keep her safe.

"Go to hell." Elizabeth tossed the gun into her opposite hand and swung up as hard as she could. Metal met flesh and bone of the shooter's left zygomatic, and he stumbled back. The pressure released off her broken wrist, but as long as adrenaline pumped through her veins, she could deal with the pain. She pushed to her feet and pumped her legs hard. Get to Braxton. Bright green eyes widened as she raised the gun. "Move!"

Braxton raised his arms over his head and faced toward the broken driver's side window.

She pulled the trigger, and the lock of his seat belt exploded. "You're welcome."

A strong hand wrenched the gun from her hand, another latching around her throat. Air pressurized in her lungs as the shooter backed her up against the SUV then aimed the gun at her temple. "Move from the vehicle and I kill her now, Levitt."

She couldn't see Braxton, couldn't hear him over the drowning sensation threatening to pull her under, but she didn't have to. He'd promised to protect her, to fight for her, and if there was one thing she couldn't fault him for, it was that he kept his promises.

"Let her go. You and I will end this right now." Fury battered Braxton's words. The SUV door slammed closed, reverberating through her. Then footsteps. Braxton strode into her peripheral vision, hands tense at his sides. Ready for a fight. "You're not going to kill her. You need her. Otherwise you would've already done it."

Calm exhales puffed the ski mask out over the shooter's mouth. Black eyes studied Braxton as a single tear slipped from Elizabeth's left eye. He'd cut off her oxygen. She'd either pass out in a few seconds or die right here. And he knew it. He was buying his time, showing he had control. The shooter lowered the gun from her temple then aimed at Braxton. "Then I'll guess I'll have to put a bullet in you."

He pulled the trigger.

Braxton spun as the bullet made contact and fell to the ground.

The scream didn't make it out as the shooter tightened his hold around her throat. Pulling her into him, he leveled that dark gaze with hers. Sirens and flashing lights closed in on the scene. "One down, Elizabeth. How many more people are you willing to watch die before you give in?"

Her vision blurred, her body growing heavy.

He didn't wait for an answer, wrenching her forward when all she wanted to do was fight back, when all she wanted to do was get to Braxton. But fighting back put her baby at risk.

She fought to stay upright as blackness closed in at the edges of her vision. Faster than she thought possible, the shooter had shoved her into the trunk of his Mercedes. The engine growled to life as darkness consumed her.

"Call an ambulance!" Unfamiliar voices pulled him out of blackness.

Braxton shot up straight with a gasp in his throat, gravel and glass cutting into his palms. The ache in his chest burned through him, and he clamped a hand over the brand-new hole in his T-shirt and Kevlar. A groan escaped as he pushed to his feet and stumbled through the circle of civilians surrounding him. "Where is she?"

He scanned the scene as Anchorage PD and a dark SUV identical to Liz's rolled onto the scene. Vincent Kalani stepped out onto the pavement, and everything inside Braxton froze. While he'd been the one to initially put Liz in the crosshairs by leaving, the call to her burner cell had sealed the deal. None of this—the bullet graze, the crash, her kidnapping—would've happened if she hadn't picked up that call. There was only one number she'd dialed on that phone. Only one way the shooter could've gotten through to her.

Braxton closed in on the forensics expert fast. Rage pushed through him as he fisted his hands in Vincent's cargo jacket and hauled him back against the SUV. "Where is she? You're the only one who called that burner. You're the only one—"

A right hook to the face knocked Braxton off balance. Vincent straightened to his full six-foot-four frame. Violence etched deep lines into the forensic expert's expression. "The next time you come at me, you better be sure to finish the job. Understand?"

A group of Anchorage PD officers stood ready to draw their weapons around him.

"He took her. That bastard took her." Braxton ignored the pulse at the left side of his face, a combination of sweat and blood sticking to his scalp. His heart threatened to explode out of his chest. Every minute he'd been unconscious had been another minute she'd gotten farther away. Damn it. One breath, two... Reason returned in small increments as he forced his blood pressure under control. "He contacted her through her burner phone. You're the only one who had that number."

"I would never put Elizabeth in danger. I trust her with my life, and she trusts me with hers. You see, that's what a team does, Levitt. We trust each other. We risk our lives for each other." Strain tightened the cords running down Vincent's neck as he stepped closer. Thick, dark eyebrows drew together. He extracted his phone from his jacket pocket, swiping his thumb across the screen. Handing the phone off, Vincent nodded. "Take it. If we're going to find her, you've got to trust me."

Braxton took the phone, his attention immediately drawn to the blinking red dot speeding south along a map of Seward Highway. His hand tightened around the device, the back hot to the touch. Elizabeth. "You're tracking her."

"I'm tracking her earpiece. You've got a

range of ten miles. I'll take care of things here." Vincent extracted the tiny device from his ear then tossed him a set of keys, pain from the bullet flooding through Braxton as he caught them midair. Setting the earpiece in Braxton's palm, the forensics expert nodded. "Go. Get my teammate back."

Braxton pumped his legs hard and inserted the earpiece as he wrenched open Vincent's SUV door. The engine growled to life as he shoved the vehicle into Drive and jammed his foot into the accelerator. "I'm coming for you, baby, hang on."

No answer.

Seward Highway stretched out in front of him, 125 miles of majestic scenery, trailheads and a hell of a lot of places to take care of a hostage. A groan fought its way up his throat. No. Whoever this guy was, he needed Liz. Otherwise she'd already be dead. Braxton pushed the SUV harder. The shooter would keep her secluded, away from the touristy cabins along the highway. "He's not going to kill her yet."

He glanced down at the phone. Still in range. It'd be another few minutes before he caught up to the Mercedes. Every cell in his body couldn't stand to be apart from her for another second longer, but he couldn't force the SUV faster. His fingers drummed hard against the steering wheel. If her kidnapper hurt her, he'd spend the rest of his life hunting the SOB down. "Come on, come on."

"Braxton?" Her strained voice spread through him like a wildfire.

"Liz." He swallowed hard against the tightening in his throat. She was alive. "Baby, are you hurt?"

"My wrist…" A hard *thunk* registered through the earpiece. Then another. She hissed. "I think it's broken, but I'm okay. He put me in the trunk. Took the burner phone and my gun. I'm trying to kick out the taillight to see where we are."

"I'm coming for you." He glanced down at the phone's screen. The red dot blinked strong. A few more miles. That was all it'd take to have her back in his arms. He hadn't given much thought to his future. All that'd mattered when he'd come back to Anchorage was keeping her alive then moving on with his life if she decided he needed to leave. But now? There was no life without Elizabeth. And he wasn't going to lose her or their baby now. Brolin might've raised him, but Liz and baby Karina were his family now. And nobody threatened his family. He gritted his teeth, fighting against the rising pressure behind his sternum. "Save your energy. I'm tracking your earpiece. I'm not far behind."

"Braxton," she said. "If I don't make it out of this alive—"

"You will." There was no other option. He was already redlining the RPMs. If he pushed the SUV any harder, the engine would explode. His breath came too fast. His heartbeat shook behind his rib cage. Headlights blinded him from the other side of the highway as he made the last curve. Less than a mile between them. "Just keep talking. Focus on my voice, and we'll get through this. You're not going to be a vic—"

Tendrils of smoke rose from the SUV's engine, the needles in the dashboard falling no matter how hard he pushed the accelerator. Soft ticks from the engine kept rhythm with the headache at the back of his skull as Braxton jerked at the steering wheel. The vehicle slowed from ninety miles plus per hour to a mere twenty in the span of ten seconds. No, no, no, no, no. "Come on!"

"Braxton? What is it? What's wrong?" Liz's voice dropped into panic.

He pulled the SUV into the shoulder, barely able to see through the thick smoke coming out of the edges of the hood. He wouldn't make it to her—not in time. His feet hit the pavement, and he rounded to the front of the vehicle. After hauling the hood overhead, he braced himself against the white-hot temperatures as he reached for the radiator cap. Pain scalded across his hand, but he got the cap off and looked inside. Empty. Damn it. "Nothing. I'm coming for you."

He tossed the cap on top of the radiator then extracted Vincent's cell phone from the interior of the SUV. He'd trained day in and day out for this. Come hell or high water, he'd get to her. Slamming the driver's side door behind him, he checked his weapon and started running, phone in hand. The shooter might never pull over, but Braxton would never stop looking for her.

"We're slowing down." Rustling filtered through the open line as she shifted inside the trunk. Then stopped. "He's pulling off the highway. I can't tell where we are. I can't see anything."

"That's okay. I know where you are." He confirmed her location on Vincent's phone, air tight in his chest as he tried to keep his voice even. A half mile up ahead, the shooter had pulled into the trailhead for McHugh Trail, a heavily wooded and rocky journey to McHugh Peak. Without snowshoes this time of year, the bastard would have a hard time getting very deep into the wilderness with a hostage, but there were plenty of places to disappear.

Or to hide a body.

Braxton spotted a distant pair of red lights down the highway. Cliffs and trees backed against the highway on one side, Turnagain Arm on the other. Every second he lagged behind, the higher the chance he'd lose them altogether. "Listen to me. I have your location. I'm going to find you. I promised I would protect you, and I will."

A loud thud resembling the slamming of a car door reverberated into his ear.

"He's coming." She lowered her voice to a whisper, a plea on her lips. "Braxton…"

His grip tightened around the phone in his hand. His muscles burned, but he pushed the pain to the back of his mind. "I'm coming, Liz. I'll be there in two minutes. Fight back. Run if you have to. I'll find you."

The high-pitched protest of metal reached his ears. The trunk lid? Muffled static claimed his attention, an all-too-familiar voice growing louder. "You've been holding out on me." Another round of static drowned out Liz's response as though someone was handling a microphone. "Whoever this is, you think you're coming to save her. Well, I've got news for you. You're too late. Elizabeth is mine."

The deafening crunch exploded in his ear.

"Liz?" A quick glance at Vincent's phone said it all: the shooter had destroyed Liz's earpiece. And any chance he had of tracking her location. "Liz!"

Chapter Eight

Her hands shook as the shooter pulled her from the trunk of the Mercedes. He'd found her earpiece almost instantly and crushed it beneath polished shoes. No passing cars. No hikers out as the sun started to lower in the sky.

No one to hear her scream.

Rough hands maneuvered her around the car and toward the trailhead up ahead. Clear skies gave way to a few twinkling stars this far out of the city, but where Elizabeth normally would've taken a few minutes to appreciate the view, now she was being forced deeper into Alaskan wilderness. "You don't have to do this."

She didn't know what else to say as branches from pines scraped across her jacket and the exposed skin of her neck and face. He'd gone out of his way to find her. Tortured her former supervisor, hijacked Oversight's feeds, stalked her for weeks. Something deep in her gut said no matter what she said, he wouldn't listen.

"Walk until I tell you to stop." His voice remained calm, collected. Dangerous.

Her boots scuffed against rocks and downed branches along the trail. She couldn't see more than five feet in front of her. He hadn't bound her. She'd catch herself if she fell, but she couldn't do much else with her broken wrist. And running into the middle of the wilderness as temperatures dropped for the night in the middle of January would be as lethal as taking a bullet to the head. Braxton had promised he'd find her, but freezing to death out here, where he couldn't track her anymore thanks to the man with the gun pressed into her back, wasn't a chance she was willing to take. Elizabeth checked his position back over her shoulder. "You obviously plan on killing me and leaving me out here for hikers to discover later. Don't I deserve to know why?"

"You don't deserve anything but what's coming to you." He pressed the gun deeper into her back, nearly to her spine despite the padding of her coat.

Freezing air burned her nostrils the higher they climbed up the trail. What did he expect her to do, make it all the way to McHugh Peak with a bullet graze, a head injury and a broken wrist? Her lungs fought against the climb in elevation, her breaths getting shallower with each step. "The Sovereign Army took credit for the bombing at Blackhawk Security, but you've made this personal. This isn't about protecting the American population's privacy, is it? You're using an extremist group as your cover."

She was only guessing, but from his lack of response, Elizabeth bet she had hit the nail on the head harder than she'd estimated. "Somehow you figured out I'd created Oversight for the NSA and changed my name. Then you tracked me down here in Anchorage and started planning my murder." She kept pushing forward. She'd only hiked this particular trail once during one of Sullivan's mandatory wilderness survival trainings, and it was difficult to decipher their location along the trail as shadows crept across the path, but there should be a branch heading off soon. At least a place she could gain the higher ground. She couldn't fight him physically, but she could disorient him long enough to buy herself time to run back toward the trailhead.

Toward Braxton.

"Why go through the trouble?" she asked.

"That's far enough." How the man determined to kill her breathed through the thick ski mask over his face, she had no idea. She chanced another glance behind her. The effect of his pressed suit combined with the mask chased a tremor down her spine. Like Death coming to collect the next soul in his cross-hairs. Too bad she'd sold her soul to the father of her unborn child a long time ago.

She stopped in her tracks, about four feet ahead of him. Her pulse beat hard at the base of her throat. The only people who knew about her facial recognition program worked for the NSA or in the Oval Office. Which meant the shooter had either hacked his way into the NSA servers—which was unlikely given she'd set up the latest security—or he'd worked for them. Then again, he'd hijacked Oversight's feeds. Or he had a partner. Her toes tingled, going numb from the dropping temperatures. If he wasn't going to kill her soon, the wil-derness would. Elizabeth wiggled her fingers to keep the circulation flowing. She strained to hear footsteps—anything—that indicated someone was coming. A hiker, police. Brax-ton. The man had a gun aimed at her, and there was nothing Elizabeth could do. "Is this where they're going to find my body?"

Keep him talking. Keep him distracted.

A gloved hand gripped her arm and spun

her around, and her breath caught in her throat. Those dark eyes seemed black now with only muted sunlight coming through the trees. His hold on her hurt, bruised. "You're trying to stall, but it won't work. I've been waiting for this day for too long."

Without hesitation, the shooter hauled her off the worn path into shadowed darkness of thick pines and underbrush. Thorns pulled at her jeans and boot laces, but he dragged her along with ease. Dry branches cracked under her boots as they got farther from the trail. Nobody would think to look for her out here. Nobody would find her.

Trees thinned ahead. The muffled sound of passing cars grew louder. He wasn't going to leave her for a hiker—or worse, her team—to find. Elizabeth swallowed hard as they cleared the tree line. The cliff rushed up to meet her before she was ready. Her heel slipped off the edge, her knees buckling as panic spread through her. Loose rocks and dirt cascaded down below onto Seward Highway, but she never saw them land. Too far down. Only the shooter's tight grip on her arm kept her from falling, but she had a feeling that anchor wouldn't last long. Her breath lodged in her chest. She couldn't take her eyes off the black ocean of pavement a few hundred feet below where he intended to let her drown. Gravity pulled at her, but she fought against it.

"Tell me why. You've tried to blow me up, tried to shoot me on more than one occasion now." She didn't dare move, didn't dare face him for fear of taking the wrong step. She wasn't a profiler like Kate, she wasn't trained to read people, but the gunman at her back had certainly made this personal. He wanted her dead, wanted revenge. There was only one reason a man acted so passionately. "There has to be a reason."

"Give me the override password to Oversight's security and I'll make this quick." The slight exhale from behind her barely reached her ears over the sound of passing cars below. Silence settled. His voice became rough, fierce, as her arm tingled from her cut-off circulation. He placed his mouth against her ear. Too close. Intimate. She closed her eyes against the flood of nausea taking hold. "Or I can draw this out until you're begging me to end you."

That was why he hadn't killed her yet. While he might've been able to reroute the feeds, he hadn't been able to get past Oversight's security to operate the program himself. Her insides suddenly felt hollowed out, the rest of her body heavy. Her heartbeat echoed through her. The work she had done for the NSA haunted her every time she closed her eyes at night. She never should've agreed to build that damn program. Never should've let them use it before it was ready. The secrets, the lies, the deaths. Oversight saved lives, but at what cost? Elizabeth licked at dry lips, the dropping temperatures wicking moisture from her mouth. Opening her eyes, she internally braced herself. "It won't do you any good. The password is only the first level to gaining control. You won't be able to hack the second. Not without me."

And not without a retinal scanner.

"Then this is going to be a long night for you." The slightest movement at her back threatened to launch her over the side of the cliff. "You know a person can sustain a three-story fall and live to tell about it. But not much else. You see, your body will be so broken, you'll never be able to do more than blink from your hospital bed until you finally give up on life." He jerked her against him then maneuvered her closer to the edge. "So save us both the time. You have five seconds to give me the password."

The back of her heel slipped off the edge of the cliff, and she held on harder to the man threatening to throw her over the edge. Panic consumed her. Her breath came quick. Her heart rate rocketed into dangerous territory. She didn't want to die. Elizabeth squeezed her eyes tight, fought to keep her balance. One wrong step. That was all it would take and everything would be over. Her stomach pitched as her mind put on a nausea-inducing slideshow of what that meant. She'd never meet her baby girl. Never protect another client. Never take control of the life she wanted.

"Two seconds," he said.

Braxton.

His name slipped between the layers of panic and demanded her attention. Her heart rate dropped, the flush of cold sweats dissipating. She opened her eyes. Fighting to breathe through a rush of dizziness, she shook her head. The shooter wouldn't be able to get past the second level of security. Not without her. So if giving him the password saved her life—saved her baby's life—there wasn't much to think about. "All right!" She licked at dry lips. "The password is 'Inicial Lake,' from my favorite TV show."

His laugh slithered down her spine.

"Your government turned its back on you the same as they did me. Tell me, *Sprinkles*," he said. "How does it feel turning your back on them now?"

"Don't call me that." Something shot down her spine, like an electric shock. Her fingers tightened as fury exploded through her. Elizabeth dug her heels into the dirt and shoved back into his chest. Her momentum knocked him off balance, but his grip still around her arm pulled her down with him. The tree line blurred in her vision as they rolled, locked around one another, in a fight for the gun. A scream worked up her throat as her already broken wrist sandwiched between them, the gun's barrel pointing straight at her forehead. He was stronger, so much stronger, than she was. But she wasn't going to die out here.

She slammed into a nearby pine, bark and dried needles scratching the skin along the back of her neck. A wave of dizziness unbalanced her as she tried to stand. The shooter fought to straighten, the gun missing from his hand.

There. Discarded in a bed of pine needles and leaves, the weapon stood out against the washed-out foliage and ice. Elizabeth lunged, but she wasn't fast enough. A leather-gloved hand wrapped around her ankle, and she hit the ground hard. Clawing at the ground, she fought to reach the gun. Dirt worked under her fingernails, but she didn't care. Without that gun, she was dead.

The shooter pulled her back against him, the weapon farther out of reach than before, and flipped her onto her back. She kicked at him, punched. He was too strong. That same gloved hand wrapped around her throat for a second time and squeezed. She clamped one hand around his wrist as leverage, trying to get oxygen, and reached for his left eye with the other despite her broken wrist.

"Get the hell away from her." Braxton's voice pierced through the darkness. She fought to scream though no sound left her mouth. The few stars above transformed into indistinct balls of light as Braxton raised his own weapon, taking aim. "Or I put a bullet in your head."

"I SAID GET away from her." Braxton widened his stance, pulling his shoulders back to make himself a smaller target. Pure rage filled his lungs, pure fire burning through his veins. Didn't matter the sun had dipped below the trees. He'd rip this SOB apart blind for coming after Liz. Family wasn't who he'd been born with. It was who he'd die for, and he sure as hell was ready to die right here, right now for the mother of his child if that was what fate held for him. But he wouldn't make it easy, either. He motioned the bastard up with the barrel of the gun.

The shooter released his grip around Liz's throat, and she fell back against the dead pine needles and foliage. Her gasps reached his ears, but Braxton never took his attention off the man standing above her. "You're nothing but a disgraced analyst, Levitt. You might've put on some muscle. Learned some fancy new moves, right? But I've been doing this for years. You can't stop me."

A smile curled at one edge of his mouth. Braxton tossed the gun, his fingers contracting into the center of his palms. Adrenaline dumped into his blood and hiked his pulse higher as he relaxed his stance. "Why don't we find out?"

The shooter took that as his cue, pulling a blade from an ankle holster. Her attacker headed straight for him, that mask still in place.

Braxton met him halfway, the small amount of sun providing enough light for him to make the first strike. The shooter lunged for him blade first. Catching the operative's wrist, he hauled the blade upward and swept the shooter's legs out from under him. They hit the ground hard, the air crushed from his lungs. His elbow made contact with the shooter's sternum, and the knife flipped into the underbrush. Out of the corner of his eye, Liz turned over onto her stomach, struggling to her feet. She searched for something in the grass. Maybe a weapon.

The shooter took advantage of the distraction and wrapped a forearm around Braxton's neck, his back pressed against the bastard's chest, and squeezed. His heartbeat pulsed hard at the base of his throat and grew louder in his ears. He leveraged his fingers between his own neck and his attacker's forearm and took a single deep breath. "Give it up, Levitt. You can't save her. Not this time."

Liz was the one he'd lived for. And he'd fight for her until the end.

A growl resonated through him. Braxton shot his knee directly back into the shooter's face, and the SOB's grip disappeared. He rolled out of range then pushed to his feet, fists up. The shooter closed in on him before he could take his next breath. He blocked the first punch. Blocked the second. But a hard kick to Braxton's sternum sent him sprawling head over heels through the dirt. Dead pine needles and something wet clung to his clothing. He forced himself to his feet as the shooter went for Liz again.

"Braxton!" She threw her hands out behind her as she backed herself toward the tree line, those mesmerizing brown eyes wide and filled with terror.

Braxton closed the distance between them, fisting the shooter's suit in his hand, and shoved a boot to the back of the operative's knee. He followed through with a punch to the face for good measure. His muscles ached, his head pounding hard from the accident. Blood still clung to the side of his face and wouldn't come off with the swipe of the back of his hand. Didn't matter. Getting Liz out of here. Protecting their baby. Ending this sick game. That was all that mattered.

The shooter went down, narrowly missing Braxton's boot to his face as he rolled. A glint of sunlight flashed before the assailant came at him with another blade. Damn it. How many other weapons was the bastard hiding in that suit? They faced off again. Hard exhales and the faint hooting of an owl cut through the groan of dodging the knife. Black eyes locked on him as Braxton sank lower into his stance. "Not just an analyst after all. Where was this fire when you practically begged me to take the intel on Oversight four months ago?"

Braxton straightened a fraction of an inch. Four months ago. The night he'd left his entire future asleep in his bed and walked away. The anonymous transaction had saved Liz's life, but how many others had been destroyed because of his moment of weakness? His attention shot to Liz as she sank to her knees near the tree line, out of hearing range, seemingly out of energy. She couldn't find out the truth. Not yet. Not when they were so close to moving on from the past. Not when the chance of them being a family—a real family—stared back at him through her eyes. "You."

"Me." The shooter rushed forward, knife up. He used the blade as a distraction, hiking a knee into Braxton's rib cage.

Bone crunched under Braxton's fist as he slammed his knuckles into the assailant's face. Once. Twice. A muffled scream escaped from the shooter's mouth underneath the mask as he swung the blade down. Agony washed over Braxton as metal met flesh. Blood dripped onto his shoelaces, the sensation of small taps against the tops of his boots the only indication of how deep the laceration went. He suppressed the scream working up his throat. No telling how fast he was losing blood without being able to take his eyes off the shooter, but the faster his heart beat, the more blood he lost. With a single punch to the shooter's midsection, Braxton used the same distraction technique to reach for the blade. He wrapped his hand around the bastard's wrist and twisted the shooter's arm until the second blade fell to the ground. His opponent dropped to one knee as Braxton forced the arm backward. "You will never lay another finger on her as long as I'm around."

Wide eyes comprehended Braxton's next thought.

"Braxton, no!" Liz's voice fought to penetrate through the haze of violence consuming him. Then her shaking fingers slid over his left shoulder. She tightened her grip on him, her fingernails digging into his flesh, her voice strained. "You can't kill him."

One kick to the sternum. That was all it would take to end this nightmare, to ensure Liz never discovered the truth about the deal he'd made. But...he couldn't do it. Not when she expected him to be the good guy, to take the higher ground. "He's not going to stop."

"He'll pay for what he's done," she said. "The bomb, the shooting in the garage, the shooting in the park and kidnapping me. He's going to spend the rest of his life behind bars. But if you kill him now, you'll be on the run for the rest of your life. And you'll be no better than him."

Braxton let go of the SOB's wrist. The shooter lost his balance, hands desperately seeking something—anything—to grab on to. He came precariously close to toppling over the edge, but Braxton reached out, gripping the bastard's suit jacket, and hauled him away from the edge. He should've felt relief. Should've been able to release the tightness building behind his sternum. But Braxton knew the truth. This wasn't over. Wouldn't be as long as the operative's heart was still beating. "Don't make me regret not killing you."

"He'll never be able to touch me from behind bars. And he's going to have to live with that knowledge until he dies." Liz's grip softened as she raised a gun and took aim. The weapon shook in her hand and, for the first time, Braxton took his attention off the shooter to look at her. Muted sunlight highlighted the sheen of sweat between her brows as she fought to keep her eyes open. She struggled to straighten fully, free hand clutched around her lower abdominals.

"Liz?" Something was wrong. Braxton released his grip on the shooter, panic coursing through every cell in his body as he reached for her. "Liz—"

Her pupils rolled up behind her eyelids as she collapsed. Braxton caught her before she hit the ground, her skin cold and waxy. Pain shredded through his injured arm under the pressure, but he didn't give a damn. Something dark and sticky stained the arm of her coat. Blood. But not enough for her to lose consciousness. Something else was wrong.

A long shadow cast darkness across Liz's features as the shooter straightened. "Looks like my job here is done, after all."

Before Braxton had a chance to stand, the bastard jumped off the edge of the cliff.

Pressure built in his lungs, crystallized puffs forming in front of his lips. What the hell?

Liz. He had to get Liz out of here. Digging his heels into the ground, he tipped her back against his injured arm and used every ounce of strength left to stand. Her thready pulse beat in rhythm to the pounding at the base of his skull. "Hang on, baby. I'm going to get you help."

Pines clawed at him as he ran straight back down the small path he'd used to find her. Another dose of adrenaline flooded through him, but the human body couldn't live off the fight-or-flight response forever. He'd crash soon. But he'd sure as hell get Liz help first. The last remnants of sunset lit the path as he took a sharp left. Rocks and twigs fought to trip him as he descended down to the trailhead. He wasn't going to lose her. Not now.

Not ever. He hit the trailhead, nearly sprinting toward the shooter's abandoned Mercedes. The sight of the car alone was enough to push him harder.

He set her down then wrenched the back passenger door open, laying her across the back seat. Framing her jawline between his thumb and first finger, he swept a strand of hair away from her face. "Almost there, Sprinkles. Don't you dare give up now. Fight. Listen to my voice and open your eyes, baby."

No answer.

Braxton climbed from the car, rounding to the driver's side door. And froze, hand on the door handle. The cliff where he'd fought the shooter fifty feet above claimed his attention. He checked the pavement below. That was the same plateau where the shooter had jumped. The hairs on the back of his neck rose on end as he studied the rest of the highway.

So where was the body?

Chapter Nine

"He shouldn't have been able to find me." New name, birth certificate, driver's license, Social Security number, credit cards, established social media accounts. She'd done everything aside from getting plastic surgery. Even with full access to her program, the shooter shouldn't have been able to track her down. At least, not without help. Oversight ran off federal databases, and everything there said she was Elizabeth Dawson. Plain and simple. She'd made sure before terminating her contract with the NSA.

The IV in the top of her hand tugged at her attention, cold fluid working through her veins. Braxton had gotten her to the hospital two days ago, but according to him, the nightmare was far from over. The shooter had jumped off that cliff he'd meant to use as her final resting place, but his body hadn't been recovered. He was still out there. Hunting her. "I changed my name. I relocated."

"Why didn't you tell me?" Sullivan Bishop had taken the seat beside her bed. Protection detail, he'd said. Her boss hadn't taken any of his own cases since taking down one of the most trained stalkers in Anchorage history—his brother. So why was he really here? The former SEAL centered that sea-blue gaze on her, and everything in her heated. Not from attraction—Sullivan had the best damn army prosecutor in the country waiting for him up the road at Joint Base Elmendorf-Richardson—but from embarrassment. "I told you when I hired you, we'd have your back. No matter what, but that comes with conditions, Liz. We're a team. I can't expect my team to function if my operatives are keeping secrets from me."

"I came to Anchorage to start over. I'd left that part of my life behind. I didn't see any reason to fill you in because none of this was supposed to happen." But hadn't she'd always known this day would come? Always looking over her shoulder for those green eyes she hadn't been able to forget. Didn't matter where she'd gone. Braxton would've found her sooner or later. "How is Braxton?"

"The nurses threatened to strap him down

if he didn't let them stitch his arm. Knowing what little I do about him, he'll barge through that door any moment to get to you." Sullivan's five o'clock shadow shifted as the small muscles along his jaw flexed. He crossed his arms, massive muscles fighting to free themselves from the signature black T-shirt he always seemed to wear. "He said the shooter jumped off that cliff edge, but neither Vincent nor the crime scene unit have been able to recover a body or any evidence the bastard got up and walked away. Do you trust him?"

Wasn't that the million-dollar question? Elizabeth pressed the edge of the bedsheet under her fingernail. She had no doubt Braxton would do what it took to protect her. Even if that meant neutralizing the threat after she'd passed out from the cramping in her abdomen. Snapping her gaze to her boss, she pressed her shoulder blades into the pillows behind her. "It's complicated."

"What about the pregnancy? When were you going to tell me about that?" he asked.

Elizabeth swallowed against the bruising around her throat, the rising rhythm of her heartbeat registering on the monitor beside her. The pain she'd experienced on that cliff, the sensation of building pressure… She'd feared the worst as Braxton raced her to the hospital. When the doctor had wheeled in the ultrasound machine, she'd expected for him to tell her the baby was gone. But baby Karina's heart beat strong. Her lower lash line burned as relief still coursed through her. "To be fair, I only told the father three days ago."

"Braxton," he said.

"Yes. What…what happened between us happened before I came to Anchorage, but I only found out about a month ago. I swear I didn't know I was pregnant when you hired me." She focused on a stray thread trying to escape from the white hospital blanket. She licked dry lips as she fought against the memories of Braxton on that cliff, of the shooter's blade cutting through him. He risked his life—yet again—for her. He'd saved her. And she wasn't sure that was something she could ever pay back. Elizabeth moved her hand over the baby. At least, not without letting him back in her life permanently. She forced herself to level her chin with the floor. To prove she could. Her baby wasn't a mistake. She was, however, a surprise Elizabeth hadn't been counting on when she'd taken on her share of clients for the firm. Her work had been the only thing keeping her sane these last few months. But if her withholding information from her boss lost her this job, she wasn't sure what she'd do. Where she'd go. "If you're worried whether or not I'll be able to protect my clients—"

"I'm not." Sullivan leaned back in his chair. "You're one of the best operatives I have. And if you feel you can still do your job while carrying this baby, I trust your judgment to know what you can handle." He ran a hand down his five o'clock shadow, the sound of short whiskers against his fingers louder than she expected. "What I am worried about is the people who blew up my conference room trying to get to you, and what they're going to do next."

"Is that why you're in here and Glennon is standing outside my room?" The Sovereign Army had taken credit for the bomb at Blackhawk Security three days ago, but now she wasn't so sure they were actually responsible. Wasn't sure they were even aware they'd been pulled into the shooter's game. What had he said? A headache pulsed at the base of her skull. The memories had gone fuzzy when she'd lost consciousness.

"I don't know much about your work for the NSA, but I've seen groups like this before, and they're not the kind of people who take government involvement in their lives lightly. For whatever reason, you're their main target."

Sullivan sat forward, elbows on his knees, the butt of his favored .40 Smith & Wesson swinging forward from his shoulder holster.

"It's not them." Elizabeth had no doubt in her mind. "The man who shot at me in the parking garage after the explosion was the same one who kidnapped me off Seward Highway. I wouldn't be surprised if he used their cause to throw me off the trail. He's coming after me by himself. It's personal for him."

Elizabeth struggled to sit up without putting pressure on her broken wrist, now in a cast. Her throat tightened. The NSA had run dozens of missions with Oversight after she'd left. Some successes. Some failures. Hundreds of lives had been affected. Every family member, friend and radicalized militant involved could have reason to hunt her down for the program's creation alone. Add losses to that number? There were too many suspects to count. "He's doing this out of revenge."

"Well, that changes things." Sullivan's eyebrows pulled together, deepening three distinct lines in the middle. "Do you know who it is? Did you get a good look at the guy?"

"No. He wore a mask the entire time we were together." Flashes of those dark eyes ma-

terialized when she closed her eyes. She shook her head. "But I'm going to find out."

"And we'll be there every step of the way if you need us," Sullivan said. "On one condition."

Her stomach tightened.

Blackhawk Security's CEO shifted forward in his chair, his attention on her. "I want to know who I really hired."

She couldn't keep the truth from him or her team any longer.

"My real name is Elizabeth Bosch. I was born in the smallest town you can imagine in the middle of nowhere, Montana. My parents ran the ski resort there, and that's basically all I can tell you about them." Only the memories of photographs came to mind now. Elizabeth trapped air in her lungs, firming her lips. How long had it been since she'd given up her secret? Four, five months? "They died when I was four. My aunt came to live with me after that, and the minute I graduated high school, I got out of there as fast as I could and haven't looked back."

"And your work with the NSA?" he asked.

"Two years ago, I was working for a start-up company, programming and piloting unmanned drones for their military contracts, when one day…" Elizabeth picked at her

chipped nail polish. She was unraveling at the seams, starting with her pathetic chipped, dirt-caked nails. "A man named Dalton Meyer approached me. He said one of his analysts had been keeping an eye on my career and thought I would be the best person for a job they had in mind. The analyst was Braxton. He offered me a contract so I could get the chance to serve my country in a bigger capacity. Turned out, the NSA wanted me to create a facial recognition program called Oversight to identify possible threats across the country. Anything from small-time crime to terrorist plots. And I did. Utilizing surveillance cameras, news coverage, phone cameras, social media, you name it, the program uses that information to predict threats." Her mouth dried. "But I ended up terminating my contract after Oversight's first trial run." She fought to breathe evenly. "Creative differences."

Movement on the other side of the single window to her room raised the hairs on the back of her neck. She didn't have to look at the man trying to force his way past Glennon at the door. Every cell in her body recognized every cell in his. Had since the day she'd met him. Would that ever change?

Door hinges protested loudly. Then he was

there. Braxton was there, and she fought back the burn in her eyes from the pure relief rushing through her. "Hey."

"Hey." Goose bumps prickled along her arms. Bruises decorated his face, scratches cutting into his jawline. Proof he'd fought like hell on that cliff. For her. Silence settled between them. Comfortable. Electrically charged.

Sullivan stood and headed toward the door. "I can tell this is going to get awkward real fast, so I'm going to leave, but Liz—" He spun around, pinning her against the hospital bed with that hard sea-blue gaze. "Never withhold intel from your team again. Got it?"

She nodded. "Got it."

"Good. Call if you need something." The former SEAL maneuvered around Braxton without a word then shut the door behind him.

Braxton dropped a black duffel bag and closed the space between them. His bandaged fingers threaded through her hair at the back of her neck then pulled her into him. Right where she belonged. He tilted her head up and kissed her. Slow at first, then with more pressure, harder, as though he thought he'd never get the chance to kiss her again. Which he almost hadn't. If it hadn't been for him... If he hadn't come for her...

A dull ringing filled her ears as she fought to catch up with her shallow breathing. The monitors beeped rapidly a few feet away, and she couldn't help but laugh. Because if she didn't allow herself this small release, she might've shattered completely. Elizabeth pulled back but kept her undamaged hand gripped in his shirt. Meeting those compelling green eyes, she tugged him down onto the bed beside her. "Take me home."

WHEN A PHOENIX rose from the ashes, she was more beautiful and stronger than ever before. And, damn, he couldn't stop stealing glances at Liz as she rested her head against the window. She'd faced death and survived. How many others could say the same?

The stitches in his arm stretched tight beneath the gauze, but he pushed the discomfort aside, attention on the all-too-familiar road. A light dusting of snowflakes fell across the windshield, but it wasn't enough to detract from the intense hollowness setting up residence in his gut. Silent seconds stretched into minutes as Liz closed her eyes.

The baby was okay. Seeing their daughter on the ultrasound, hearing her tiny heartbeat. It was as though a dam had been destroyed and a flood of emotions had washed forward.

He'd nearly sank to his knees right there in the middle of the hospital room. And in that moment, he'd allowed himself to imagine things he hadn't before. Meeting his daughter for the first time, celebrating her first birthday, sending her off to kindergarten, walking her down the aisle on her wedding day. The three of them—him, Liz and Karina—together as a real family.

Slush splashed up onto the windshield, bringing him back to the moment. He'd forfeited those fantasies the night he'd walked out on Liz after they'd conceived their baby. Forfeited his right to happiness. His right to ask her for the possibility of a future between them—wouldn't work. Not with the NSA dead set on putting him behind bars for treason. He couldn't ask her to wait, to hope.

Braxton tightened his grip on the steering wheel of another Blackhawk Security SUV, fighting back dark memories of tearing down Seward Highway in pursuit of saving her life in another vehicle exactly like this. He might've forfeited everything that night, but he'd do whatever it took to keep his girls safe. No matter the cost.

Soft snoring filled the interior of the vehicle, and he looked over to see Liz's lips slightly parted, her features slack. As much as he'd been able to research during the last two days of her in the hospital, the first few months of pregnancy were the most exhausting. Keeping up with a growing fetus took a toll he could only imagine. But fending for her life on top of that? Liz deserved to climb under the covers of the nearest bed and never climb out. He could give her that. If only for a few days.

He turned into a long asphalt driveway, and his gut clenched. A gallery of pines lined the property of the forty-year-old, two-story home. Wood-paneled siding and a contemporary design helped the cabin stand out against the others in the area, the nearest a quarter mile away. Typical cabins out here had been designed with winter months in mind, but not this one. The flower boxes still attached under the first-story windows and the long expanse of grass leading to the backyard paid homage to the past best left forgotten, but he didn't know where else to go.

Home sweet home.

The shooter had gotten away. Braxton didn't know how. He only knew that bastard had put Liz in his sights. And Braxton's gut said he wouldn't stop until the job was done. But they would be safe here. Then he'd move them to another safe house. And another.

He'd move her around the entire country if it meant keeping her alive until they had a lead on the man hunting her. Braxton turned off the engine, the keys jingling against his leg. Reaching out, he slid his beaten knuckles along her cheekbone and lowered his voice. "We're here."

"Five more minutes." She buried herself deeper in her coat, the one arm still torn from the bullet graze at the park. White gauze lay at the bottom of the hole covering a row of stitches. "Too tired to move."

A laugh escaped through his nose. He dropped the keys into his jacket pocket and shouldered the door open. Rounding to the front of the SUV, he fought the urge to burn the entire cabin to the ground and walk away before she had a chance to step a foot inside. Leave the memories in the ashes. A gust of fresh, chilled breeze cleared his head. Get her inside. Keep her safe. He carefully opened the passenger side door, a smile thinning his mouth as she caught herself tipping out. "I can help with that."

"Haven't you done enough?" She slid her hands up his forearms for balance. Despite the freezing temperatures, he didn't feel the cold. Not with her in his arms. Then again, she'd always made him run hot. Her feet hit the pavement, but Liz didn't make any move to free herself of his hold. "You know, saving my life and all. That one time."

The smile stretching across her face was enough to stop his blood pumping. If it weren't for the thin scratches, the bullet graze at the top of her arm, the broken wrist and the four stitches in her hairline, it would have. But knowing she'd almost died because of him, because he'd left her unprotected all these months, had twisted him into a sick mess. He slid his hand into hers, locking her against him. "Let's get you inside."

She studied the cabin for the first time, it seemed. Took in the wide expanse of windows at the front, the balcony hanging over the covered patio, the line of trees threatening to overtake the roof at any moment. "Another one of your safe houses?"

"No." He took a deep breath, leading her to the sidewalk and toward the front door. He'd told her about his past. Told her about his family, about how Brolin Levitt had lost this same exact cabin to the bank after he decided his addiction was more of a priority than paying the mortgage. Braxton tightened his grip around her hand. It'd taken a lot of negotiation under a fake name with the couple who'd purchased the home after his parents had been foreclosed on, but something inside him hadn't been able to let it go. Now he knew why he'd kept it around for so long. To keep her and their baby safe. "It's the cabin I grew up in."

"You bought it?" She followed him along the sidewalk, past the crack near the front steps where he'd tripped and broken his arm when he was ten. Past the large pile of firewood he'd been chored with stocking most summers before they hit the wooden steps leading to the front door. "Why?"

"For you." Wood protested under their weight as he climbed the nine steps it took to reach the threshold of his childhood. All in all, his family had had happy memories in this place. His parents had bought the cabin right after finding out they were pregnant with their one and only son. Brolin had been manager of a bank then, and Karina had stayed home to raise Braxton. He dug for his keys then inserted the key into the dead bolt and turned. That'd been before Brolin's addiction destroyed everything Braxton had ever known.

A rush of cinnamon-and-apple-scented air slammed into him as he pushed the door open. With Liz's hand still wrapped around his, he led her inside. The crew he'd hired to gut the insides had done a damn fine job.

New white tile in the entryway, the perfect color of hardwood flooring off to the left in the living room, peach walls the same exact color as he remembered, only fresher. Windows let in natural light from nearly every angle imaginable, welcoming him home. But Braxton couldn't move. How long had it been since he'd stepped through that door? Twenty years? The house had gone through a lot since then. He'd gone through a lot.

"What do you mean, for me? When did you buy it?" Liz studied the gleaming tile, the sparse furniture, the hallway leading straight back to the renovated kitchen.

"Last year, when I realized I wanted to be more than your friend." When he'd realized he'd fallen in love with the woman who'd sat less than five feet from his cubicle. He didn't dare look at her as he tugged her toward the stairs off to the right and up to three massive bedrooms for her to choose from, two smaller, one master. Beds and bathrooms for each. Braxton slowed down at the top of the stairs but didn't dare drop her hand. Not yet. Not when she was the only thing keeping him anchored in the present. "Have your pick. We're going to be here for a few days."

"Where did you set up your surveillance?" she asked.

"In that one. My old room." He led her to the right, stopping under the door frame as he pushed the door wider. After the renovations, he barely recognized it. No posters from his favorite band, no dartboard, no toys and action figures. Just peach-colored walls, a window with blackout curtains, a king-size bed with new bedding and a desk with his surveillance systems. Braxton leaned his weight into the door frame. "The other bedrooms won't have the glow from the monitors keeping you up."

"I don't mind." Liz dropped his hand. She moved inside, taking in the room, and sat on the edge of the bed. Dropping her coat beside her, she looked completely at ease despite the bruises and scratches marring her perfect skin. Now fully lit from the natural light coming through the window, he noted the dark circles under her eyes, the lack of color in her lips, the slight tremor in her hands. He'd seen her like this before. Only once, after Oversight's real-world test run in which a CIA agent had lost his life. She'd tried not to internalize that guilt, but he'd read it on her face that day, and it'd taken one night of him finally getting the guts to kiss her senseless until she forgot. The same night he'd gotten her pregnant. The same night he'd disappeared. "I want to be able to see him coming."

His gut sank. Damn it. He should've thrown the SOB who'd taken her off the cliff like he'd planned. He could've ended this nightmare. Could've brought her some justice. He pushed off the wall, closing the space between them. Crouching in front of her, he fought the urge to use the same tactics he had the night they'd been together that single time. "Liz—"

"I don't need you to talk." Framing his jawline with her hands, Liz pulled him closer and crushed her mouth against his. A burst of her lavender scent destroyed the wall of care he'd put in place for her. She swept her tongue past his lips, and his knees hit the hardwood. No matter how much muscle he'd put on, no matter how many hours he'd trained, none of it stood against her. Pressing his palms against the small of her back, he took anything he could get from her and more. Then she pulled away. "I need you to stay with me tonight."

Chapter Ten

She didn't want to think about the explosion. Not the shooting in the garage, her kidnapping. The fact she'd very nearly been thrown off a cliff and was still the center of a hit man's plans for revenge. None of it. The only thing Elizabeth focused on now was him. All she wanted in this moment was him. His five o'clock shadow prickled against her palms as she framed his jawline. Seconds passed. A minute?

He backed away from her, those green-gray irises widening as his pupils shrank.

Confusion gripped her hard. "Say something."

"You don't want me to stay with you…not right now." His phone chimed, but Braxton didn't move. He looked over her, her skin burning everywhere his gaze made contact. Raising his hand, he slid his fingertips up her arm and rested his thumb against the hollow at the base of her throat. The tendons along his neck ticked. "I promised to protect you and failed. I should've gotten to you sooner."

"I'm perfectly capable of deciding what I want for myself. I know exactly what I'm asking you to do." Low-grade pain spread from the bruise around her neck. Elizabeth automatically swallowed against the tightness overtaking her entire body, but instead of flinching, she reached out for him. Fisting her fingers in his long-sleeve T-shirt, she tugged him into her, where he belonged. Tendrils of his hair hid half of his face from her, and she brushed them out of the way with her casted hand, refusing to think of how she'd ended up with the broken wrist in the first place. "I'm alive, Braxton. We survived. And we'll keep surviving as long as we're together. So don't get any bright ideas about pulling away now."

"You should've let me kill him." His voice dropped into dangerous territory, but this had a new edge to it. So sharp it threatened to cut straight through her. The Braxton she remembered vanished as steel hardened his expression. "I could've ended this once and for all."

"Ended this." The words were more for herself than for him. The bullet wound in her arm burned, her muscles wound tight with strain and overuse. But none of that compared to the sinking of her stomach from a combination of the guilt etched into his features and the disappointment consuming her. He blamed himself for the events of the last few days— that was clear—but what he should be worried about was the baby he'd helped conceive. About whether or not he was going to fight to stay in her life. "I know you'd do anything to protect me and this baby, but killing him would've put you back on the NSA's radar. Self-defense or to save me. It wouldn't matter. They would've taken you, and I'd never see you again."

"Wasn't that my end of our deal?" he said.

Silence settled between them as reality closed in. Yes. Back in the garage, before he'd given her a glimpse of how thoughtful he was, how caring, before he'd risked his life to save hers, she'd made him swear to crawl back to the rock he'd been hiding under for the last four months when this was over. Since he'd come back into her life, he'd gone out of his way to prove how much she'd meant to him. The ice cream and sprinkles, the nicknames, the slight lift of his lips when he looked at her, the undeniable physical attraction they shared. Or had it all been an act? A way to force her to accept his protection in order to extinguish his own guilt for leaving? She blinked to clear her head, to build up the wall that'd been in place for so long, and shut down her initial reaction. "You're right. Killing him wouldn't have changed anything."

No response.

She released her grip on his shirt and stepped away from him. She couldn't breathe, couldn't think. Four months ago, he'd taken her to bed, given her everything she'd wanted between them, then disappeared without a word. He was the one who'd tracked her down. He was the one who'd promised to protect her. He was the one who'd kept her alive these last few days. They were having a baby together. But apparently not even the tiny creature in her uterus who'd disrupted absolutely everything could make him want to stay. Damn it, how could she have been so stupid to think this time would be different? The NSA's charges against him hadn't changed. Why would he?

"You should leave when this is over." Elizabeth maneuvered around him toward the attached bathroom. She swiped at the tears in her eyes as the peach walls and surveillance monitors blurred in her peripheral vision.

Cool air rushed against the exposed skin along her arms as she closed the bathroom door behind her. No footsteps on the other side of the door. No knock against the wood. Braxton hadn't followed her. But she wasn't sure if she'd wanted him to. Tapping the crown of her head against the door, Elizabeth steered her attention to the white, brown, tan and teal tile of the soaking tub. What had she been thinking, asking him to stay with her tonight?

That was the problem. She hadn't been thinking. Being the center of a madman's revenge, of nearly dying not once but three times had distorted the single rule she'd set for herself when this whole thing started. Protect herself. Emotionally, physically, mentally. At whatever cost. But for the briefest of moments, he'd slid past her defenses, and she hadn't realized it until right now. For the briefest of moments, she'd let him have control.

Elizabeth forced herself to put one foot in front of the other until she'd reached the tub, and she turned the knob for hot water. To rinse some of the rawness down the drain. She undressed and added a lavender-scented soap beneath the water stream. The same brand she used at home. Wasn't surprising. Seemed Braxton had held on to a lot of things from the past. She studied the rest of the bathroom for the first time. For a while there, it seemed he'd held on to his feelings for her, too, as he'd held on to this house. But now she recognized her own wishful thinking.

He was shutting her out.

And hell, it hurt. She should've been used to that by now. She blinked back the burn in her lower lash line as the truth began to show. Stay in control. Stay strong. Whatever she imagined might happen between them was a fantasy, some twisted desire to have the support system neither of them had had growing up.

She stepped into the bath, flinching from the sting of the water on her fresh cuts, and curled in on herself. Her knees pressed against her cheeks. If the past four days had proven anything, it was that she and Braxton wouldn't work. Not with the NSA's charges over his head. Not with his flight instincts so engraved into his personal arsenal. Not when he tested everything she knew about herself.

She tightened her hold around her shins. The fact she was pregnant, the fact she'd been put in the shooter's crosshairs, was truly as bad as things could get, right? How much more pain did she have to go through before giving up was okay? Elizabeth ran a hand through her hair. No. She wouldn't give up. For the sake of her baby, she had to see this through. Even if her daughter lost a father in the process.

The doorknob clicked a split second before Braxton pushed it open. She lifted her attention toward him but didn't move. Didn't speak. She couldn't. Because the anguish etched across his expression gutted her to the bone. Green-gray eyes locked on her and, suddenly, she was losing the battle against him all over again. He heel-toed off his boots one at a time then lifted his shirt over his head. The stitches across his arm almost bore resemblance to the bullet graze across hers. He'd been through hell just as much as she had the past three days. She had to remember that. He'd risked his life for her, almost died for her.

Valleys and ridges shifted across his abdomen as he closed the distance between them. Two steps. Three. Her mouth dried as he stared down at her, his dark, fathomless eyes burning straight through her. Climbing into the tub behind her, Braxton sank beneath the water almost fully clothed. Water rushed over the edge of the tub, but she didn't have the energy to care. Traitorous, treacherous need overtook her as he slid callused palms along her shoulders and pulled her back against him. All she wanted was him. Skin against skin, she wanted to feel alive. He wrapped his arms around her and pressed his mouth to her ear. "I've got you, Sprinkles."

A shiver chased down her spine despite the warmth of the water around her and Braxton's heat at her back. The tears came then, so strong she couldn't hold them back anymore. She shook against him, and he only held her tighter. This. This was what she missed about him. Not the promises. Not the offer of ice cream or the nicknames. She'd missed being in his arms, missed knowing she had someone she could count on, if only for a night.

"And I'll never let you go." He swiped her hair out of her face and turned her onto her side. Holding her against him with one arm, he rubbed small circles between her shoulder blades. When the sobs had racked her body and the water dropped in temperature, Braxton lifted her out of the tub. Goose bumps pimpled along her skin as he carefully dried her off with a fresh towel off the rack then led her back into the bedroom without a word.

Droplets of cold water hit her skin from her wet hair as he pulled an oversize shirt and a pair of sweats out of the dresser. He helped her dress, sliding his fingers along the back of her calves and down to her Achilles' heels. Another tremor lightninged through her, one that had nothing to do with the drop in her body temperature. Once she was dressed, Braxton interlaced his fingers with hers, tugging her down onto the bed. Shedding his own clothing, he pulled a pair of sweats from the dresser and shoved his legs into them. His weight on the mattress settled against her, hiking her heart into her throat. The past four days had destroyed her inside and out. And she had nothing left to give. Not to him. Not to the man trying to kill her. Not to her team. "Braxton, I can't—"

"I don't need you to talk." Her own words to him released the anxiety climbing up her throat. He maneuvered under the covers, his heat chasing the chill from her bones, and coiled around her. His fingers encased hers against her collarbones. They hadn't solved anything, but right now, pressed against him, she didn't care. His exhales kept rhythm with hers. "I need you to go to sleep."

Exhaustion pulled her under.

THE SHRILL RING of his burner phone ripped him out of Liz's warm hold.

"What is it?" The grogginess in her voice revealed she wasn't entirely awake yet, and he smoothed his hand over her shoulder.

"Just my phone. Go back to sleep." Four hours. That was all the peace they'd gotten.

Braxton threw the covers off and collected the phone from where he'd left it on the desk with his surveillance equipment. Unknown number. Warning spread through him. He checked the monitors. No movement along the tree lines or around the house. But that didn't mean Liz's stalker hadn't found another way to get to her. Studying the steady, slow rise and fall of her shoulders, he swiped his thumb across the screen then headed for the bedroom door, closing it behind him. If the shooter had somehow gotten ahold of yet another of their burner phone numbers, she didn't need to hear the shooter's voice after what she'd been through. "Talk."

"Hello to you, too, sunshine." Vincent Kalani's voice eased some of the tension climbing up Braxton's spine. He'd handed the operative one of his old preprogrammed burners while Liz had been recovering in the hospital after they discovered cloning tech on Vincent's device, but had pushed the investigation to the bottom of his priorities. New phone. New number. No chance the shooter could listen in on their calls this time. "Guess you didn't get my message."

Memory of his phone chiming earlier—before Liz had walked away from him with tears in her eyes—rushed forward. It hadn't been important then. "Guess not. What do you have?"

"We got a hit on the fingerprints from bullet casings recovered after the shooting at Town Square," Vincent said. "I sent the report to your phone, but looks like you're not checking email right now. Is it safe to assume you two hooked—"

"Say another word and I'll change your name to Veronica Kalani in every federal database I can hack. Which is all of them." Braxton checked over his shoulder. The door to the bedroom was still closed, and he moved farther down the hallway so this conversation wouldn't wake the woman in his bed. What'd happened between them a few short hours ago, her apparent fear of him leaving again, had left him hollowed out. Useless. The dark, raging creature inside him, the one that would do anything to stay with her, even if it put her in more danger, had taken control then. And he'd been lost. Seeing her in the tub, so vulnerable, so lost… It'd broken him. He never wanted to see her that way again. Not Liz. Him leaving had been part of the deal they'd struck before the shooter had tried to take them out in the parking garage. But everything had changed since then. "What does the report say?"

"Can you really change anyone's name?" Vincent asked. "Elliot thinks I don't know he's been stealing my lunch out of the refrigerator here at the office, and I'm currently looking for ways to make him pay."

Braxton took a deep breath, running his hand over his jawline. His normally groomed five o'clock shadow had thickened over the past few days. No time to shave when a shooter had put the woman he'd die to protect in his sights. "As tempting as that sounds, let's go back to the fingerprints."

"Right. Prints match a CIA agent named Justin Valentin," Vincent said. "You heard of him?"

Braxton dropped the phone away from his ear. It wasn't possible. Justin Valentin had been the field operative killed during Oversight's test launch. None of this made sense. Had the NSA identified the wrong corpse? Had Justin survived? The moment Liz heard about the evidence… He didn't know what she'd do. Vincent's voice reached through the haze threatening to suffocate him. Raising the phone to his ear, he pinched the bridge of his nose and closed his eyes. "Are you one hundred percent sure those fingerprints match that name?"

"I ran it twice. Why?" Vincent's confusion reached through the line. "Isn't this good news? You got your man. Liz can put this behind her."

"Not in the least. Did you run a background check after you matched the prints?" If the forensics expert had, they wouldn't be having this conversation. Braxton looked up and froze. Every cell in his body caught fire at the sight of Liz staring back at him from the bedroom door. "I'm going to have to call you back." He lowered the phone again, hitting the end button.

"Vincent found something." Not a question. Liz crossed her arms over her midsection, one of her textbook moves when she slammed her invisible guard into place. Dark circles still haunted her beneath those chocolate-brown eyes, exhaustion evident in her features, but the tears were gone. She'd gotten only a few hours of sleep over the last few days. With the added strain of the baby and the stress of being kidnapped on her body, it was a wonder she was still standing. "Tell me."

"We don't have to do this now." Braxton's bare feet stuck to the cold hardwood floor as he closed in on her. "You can go back to sleep—"

"I'm fine," she said. "Just tell me."

He nodded.

"Vincent recovered bullet casings from the shooting at Town Square. He was able to match the partial fingerprints on them to a CIA agent who died last year." He opened Vincent's email on his phone and handed it to her. "He matched them to Justin Valentin."

"That's not possible." Her exhale swept over his bare neck and chest. Her voice gained strength with each word out of her mouth. "I was there where Dalton Meyer ran the trial run, Braxton. I saw Agent Valentin die on the screen right in front of me. I watched as they lowered his coffin into the ground a week later. Justin Valentin is buried in Rock Creek Cemetery in Washington, DC."

"I was there, too, remember? I know what happened." He remembered every minute. Oversight's first real-world test run would stay ingrained in his memory forever. The program had identified a group of Afghan rebels intent on taking out the US Embassy in Kabul. What the program failed to identify, however, was the CIA agent deeply implanted within the group when the order for neutralization came down from on high. Liz had told them the tech wasn't ready, but her supervisor, Dalton Meyer, hadn't listened, and an American life had been lost on the program's first test run. Liz had never forgiven herself. "Vincent ran the prints twice. Unless you've got another explanation, we need your boss and whatever connections he has to get a court order to exhume whoever is in that coffin."

"No. The shooter...whoever is doing this is trying to mess with my head." She thrust the phone back at him, not bothering to read the ballistics report. Liz ran a hand through her short hair, and she took a step back. The past three days had her spiraling and, hell, he couldn't blame her. But ever since her stalker had tried to kill her with a bomb, they'd been reacting. The explosion, the shootout in the garage, her kidnapping. It wouldn't end until Liz was dead. And that wasn't an option. Not for him. "He must've known about that mission and somehow gotten access to those confidential files. Justin Valentin is dead."

"You think Justin's prints were planted." What was the point of trying to set up a dead man? It didn't make sense.

"In the last three days, there's only been one man I know of who's trying to kill me. He's planned this out for months, if not years." Liz crossed her arms again, accentuating all the mouthwatering curves under his T-shirt. "Do you honestly believe he'd be stupid enough to leave his own fingerprints on those bullet casings where we could find them?"

Not a chance. They were dealing with a professional. No way in hell he'd leave evidence behind without reason. "How do you get a dead man's prints on a bullet casing?"

"That's the million-dollar question," she said.

Braxton checked his phone for the time. "It's too late to have Sullivan get a court order from a judge. But I'm not going to wait around for this guy to take another shot at you. We need to trace Oversight's feeds and attack him head-on."

"That's not a plan." She dropped her arms to her side. "That's a death sentence."

Frustration built. "I don't want you to spend the rest of your life looking over your shoulder, Liz. Especially not with our daughter in tow. She deserves better than that."

Liz stepped back as though she'd taken a direct hit, and his stomach dropped. Waves of pinks and greens filtered through the wide expanse of windows, highlighting the sharp angles of her features. Aurora borealis rippled across the night sky, brighter than he'd ever seen it before. "Are you willing to bet your life on that?"

"I know why you won't touch Oversight's

code, but running for the rest of your life is no way to live. I know that better than anyone." Braxton stepped into her range. He couldn't think with her so close. But he was tired of thinking. Tired of running.

"Dalton should've listened to me." Liz shook her head. "Oversight wasn't ready. I told him that the day before the scheduled trial run. I told him the programming kept skipping the background checks because of a broken line of code I hadn't been able to find, but he didn't care. A man died because of my mistake. You really want to take that risk?"

"I'll take my chances on you every day for the rest of my life." He countered her retreat, and his body temperature hiked at least two degrees. "Because of all the variables I bet the shooter calculated before making his move on you in that conference room, I know he didn't account for you fighting back."

Chapter Eleven

She'd stick to her end of the deal. Elizabeth would let him protect her until the threat was neutralized, then he could go back into hiding until the NSA forgot his name.

Her gut tightened at the thought, and she squeezed his hand draped across her hip. He'd convinced her to come back to bed, but she couldn't sleep. The sooner they ended this investigation, the sooner she'd have to watch him walk away. Again. But as much as she wanted to drown in fantasies of Braxton helping her raise this baby—of them becoming the family their daughter deserved—he couldn't stay. And the sooner she realized that, the better. For her and their baby. She trusted him enough to keep her alive. That would have to be good enough.

"You're still awake," he said.

She pressed her shoulder blades against his chest. His body heat tunneled through her borrowed sweats. What'd happened on that trail…she couldn't get that dark gaze out of her mind. "I see him when I close my eyes. I can't get him out of my head."

Braxton hiked her against him, dropping his mouth to her shoulder. "You're not responsible for any of this, Liz. This guy might be doing this out of some sick need for revenge, but I know you. You'd never deliberately put anyone in danger."

"Except I did. On the dozens of missions I let the NSA use my program." She turned her heard toward him, only the glow of the surveillance system highlighting one side of her face. "He used the Sovereign Army to take credit for the bomb, but what if this is about Oversight like we originally thought?"

"If this guy is connected to the work you did for the NSA, we'll find out who he is." He traced his fingers down her arm, coaxing goose bumps in his tracks, and placed his mouth at her ear. He slid his hand beneath the hem of her shirt, right over their growing daughter. "But right now, you and this baby have been through hell. You need to sleep."

"I can't sleep." Not when every time she closed her eyes, fear gripped her throat to the point she couldn't breathe. Elizabeth turned into him, framing one side of his jaw with her palm. His beard prickled against her skin. Images of their one night flashed through her mind. He'd been comforting her then, too, right after Oversight had failed its first test run in the field. A CIA agent had lost his life that day, the same man whose fingerprints Vincent had found on those bullet casings. Justin Valentin. And Braxton had been there for her. How many more mistakes had her program made since she'd told the NSA she'd never work for them again? How many more lives was she responsible for? She didn't want to think about it.

Four months. Such a long time, yet not long enough for her feelings to disappear as fast as he had. She hadn't expected that. That chaotic tangle of emotions should've left by now. But they hadn't. He'd become part of her a long time ago. And there weren't exactly exorcists for this kind of thing. When it came to Braxton Levitt, she had the feeling he'd never leave her system entirely. But maybe that didn't have to be a bad thing. "Where have you been all this time?"

"Everywhere. Cambodia, Taiwan, Russia. I made it a point to stick to nonextradition countries." A shiver rushed down her spine at his touch, and Braxton flashed her that gut-wrenching grin of his. "But that's not what you want to ask me, is it?"

He could read her so well. Too well. Nervous energy exploded through her. All she'd been able to think about when the shooter had held her at the edge of the cliff had been Braxton's name. She didn't have any right to ask. He'd moved on. So had she. New city, new job, new name. She'd fought to leave her old life behind, a life that had included him up until the end. But the question still nagged at her. Clenching her teeth against the oncoming disappointment, Elizabeth studied the shadows lining his collarbones. "What was…" She swallowed around the growing lump in her throat. "What was I to you?"

He set her chin between his thumb and index finger, urging her to look up. The color of his eyes was lost in the blue light of his surveillance system a few feet away, but she read every change in his expression. Because she'd learned how to read him, too. "Everything."

Her breath came too fast. Her heartbeat seemed to shake behind her rib cage. Everything she'd done to this point—refusing to work with him, laying out the rules, putting up her guard—had been to protect herself, but he'd figured out a way around all of that. He'd buried himself beneath her skin and become part of her. Would it always be like this? When the smoke cleared, could this work? When someone wasn't trying to kill her, when the NSA wasn't trying to put him behind bars for the rest of his life.

"Come here." The lines at the edges of his mouth deepened with his smile. Braxton offered her his hand, sliding off the bed when she took it. Rough calluses caught on her skin, but right now, she only had attention for the slow burn of desire swirling in his gaze.

Her bare feet hit the cold hardwood floor, and he tugged her into him. Right where she needed to be. Without letting go of her hand, Braxton turned toward the desk and pulled open the top drawer. He handed her a small glass bottle with a long neck, the weight of his attention crushing the air in her lungs. "Black fingernail polish?"

"You've been through hell the last few days." He closed the short space between them, crowding her until her knees hit the edge of the bed. Collapsing back, she held her breath as Braxton sank to his knees in front of her. He tugged her sweats up around her calves, his touch somehow hot and cold at the same time. Or had her nerve endings started playing tricks on her again? "Let me take care of you."

"You happen to have black fingernail polish on hand?" Of course he did. Just as he'd put her favorite brand of lavender soap in the bathrooms, how he'd stocked the freezer with chocolate ice cream and the drawers with rainbow-colored sprinkles. He'd gone out of his way to ensure her small comforts came first. At first, she'd thought it'd been to manipulate her, to get her to trust him again. But now? Now a familiar feeling climbed up through her insides. The feeling of falling.

"I've got supplies stashed in this house you can't imagine." He feathered his fingertips down the tight muscles in her left calf then applied pressure. Her grip tightened on the edge of the mattress as she tipped her head back against her shoulders. "We could stay here for weeks without stepping outside this bedroom."

Elizabeth leveled her gaze with his. Her leg jerked beneath his hands as he pressed into one of her more sensitive ticklish spots. A laugh burst from her between her lips. "Sorry. I don't normally let people massage my calves. I'm afraid I'll kick them in the face, I'm so ticklish."

"I'll have to remember that." Half a smile stretched his mouth thin, and her stomach shot into her throat. Setting her foot on top of his thigh, he reached for the glass bottle and twisted off the lid. In the glow of his surveillance system, he touched up the tips of her toenails effortlessly. But what couldn't he do? He'd saved her life from a gunman, tracked her down to the edge of that cliff, fought a professional shooter as though he'd trained to fight all his life, established safe houses to keep them off the grid and learned to cook a turkey and vegetable soup she still couldn't stop tasting at the back of her throat. Blowing on her wet toenails, he sat back on his heels then swung himself up to stand. "Good as new."

Elizabeth couldn't take her attention off him. Something had changed. Some defining moment had altered his life that night he'd disappeared. "The night you left. Something happened, something to make you want to change your appearance, to learn to fight, to handle a gun." Because the man she'd known had never picked up a gun in his life or learned how to throw a punch. He'd been an analyst, glued to his computer screen. "What happened to you?"

His rough exhale reached her ears. The mattress dipped under his weight as he sat beside her, elbows on his knees, the little black bottle of nail polish gripped between his hands. He nodded once. "You happened to me. I couldn't protect you then. That needed to change."

Her lips parted to ask every question running through her mind. Protect her from what? Why hadn't he told her the truth? Did it have something to do with the NSA? But did any of it matter? Not really. This moment, that was all that mattered. "Kiss me."

"Don't start something you can't finish, Sprinkles." He shifted at her side, his dark hair skimming over his shoulders. Braxton moved a strand of hair off her forehead. The past four months living off the federal government's radar had hardened his features, but she still recognized the man beneath the guarded exterior and new muscle. And she wanted him now more than ever. "I have very little control when it comes to you."

"Please. I need this." She rolled her lips between her teeth and bit down. This wasn't an attempt to get him to stay after the investigation ended. It wasn't an attempt to satisfy her own attraction. Pure, unfiltered need coursed through her. The need to be touched, to be cared for, loved, even. If only for a night. Her throat dried. Before she lost him forever. "I need you."

Braxton threaded his fingers through the

hair at the back of her neck, pulled her into him and set his mouth over hers. His clean, masculine scent clung to her borrowed clothing, to the sheets, became part of her, and she couldn't get enough. He maneuvered over her, pushing her onto her back, and slid his hand along the outer part of her thigh. He hiked her calf around his hip. Tightening her grip on him, Elizabeth breathed a bit easier despite his added weight. Patience was a virtue, but they didn't have time for that. She cocked her head to one side and opened her mouth wider for him.

Any second now reality would work its way back, but she'd stretch this night to last as long as possible. With a freshly painted set of toenails.

HE'D LIED TO HER.

The changes he'd made over the last four months hadn't been about the realization he couldn't protect her. If he'd known being part of her life would end this way, Braxton never would've recruited her for the NSA. But there was no changing the past. As for the future… Hell, he needed her as much as he needed oxygen in his lungs. And that was a very dangerous thing.

Braxton buried his nose at the crown of her

head, lavender and woman fighting to drown the guilt clawing its way through him. He should've ended it on that cliff side, gotten her free of this nightmare. Gotten her free of him. A murder charge would've kept him out of the country for the rest of his life and put a digital target on Liz's back, but at least then she'd be safe. He'd underestimated the shooter, banked on the SOB taking the intel on Oversight and staying the hell out of her life. Braxton had been wrong.

Wouldn't happen again.

Muted sunlight lit the room enough for him to make out the handle of his Glock across the room. He'd shed his shoulder holster and gun before getting in the tub with her, literally let down his guard for her. But it was time to end this. Maneuvering out from beneath Liz's warm body, trying not to wake her, he crossed the room in three steps and reached for his clothing. He'd track Oversight's feeds himself and finish this today. The bastard had tried to hurt his family, and Braxton would make him pay. He'd make sure the guy never touched her or their baby again.

He dressed fast then fastened his shoulder holster into place and collected a backpack of supplies and a secure laptop he'd stashed in the closet. Liz shifted beneath the sheets, a small moan escaping her throat as she rolled onto her side, and Braxton froze. The back-pack in his hand worked to cement him in place. As though it knew the repercussions of leaving her in the middle of the night after taking her to bed yet again. But what choice did he have? Whoever'd kidnapped her would try again. And would keep trying until her pulse stopped beating. Braxton forced him-self to breathe evenly through the thought. No. He'd end this now. He'd do what he had to, to keep her safe.

He followed the edge of the bed until he stood over her. Planting a kiss on the top of her head, he memorized the way she smelled, engraved the memories of their night together in his mind. Ran his fingers through the ends of her hair one last time. Dropping his voice, he crouched beside her and whispered more to himself than to her. "It'll always be you, Liz."

Braxton pushed to his feet, out of time, and scanned the surveillance monitors on the other side of the room before making his es-cape downstairs and toward the front door. He tossed his burner phone onto one of the couches in the living room to his right as he reached for the doorknob. He'd start with the fingerprints recovered from the rooftop shoot-ing. Justin Valentin had been buried back in

Washington, DC, but there had to be somebody—a family member, an old partner, a friend—who knew of his work for the CIA and had access to his personal belongings. The only other option was that the agent had faked his own death after Oversight's trial run. He gripped the doorknob hard as metal grew warm beneath his hand. Exhaling hard, he squeezed his eyes shut. Focus. Find the shooter. Keep Liz safe. He'd gone off the grid once, he could do it ag—

"I must be horrible in bed if you have to make a quick getaway in the middle of the night every time you sleep with me." Heat shot through him at the sound of her sleep-ragged voice. Soft footsteps padded down the stairs, but Braxton didn't dare turn around. He dropped his hand from the doorknob as Liz stopped short behind him. "But to be fair, I guess it's morning now, isn't it?"

He turned his head toward her. "Liz—"

"Don't worry, Braxton. I'm not mad." Her voice hollowed. "In order to be mad, you'd have to disappoint me in some way, which implies I had expectations. And I didn't. I knew you'd have to leave." She studied him. "But for the record, you don't have a promising future in clandestine work. You're the noisiest dresser on the planet."

"I can end this." The muscles down his spine tensed, ready for battle. "I can make sure he never comes after you again."

"What happened to us ending this together?" Liz circled into his line of sight. Exhaustion played a wicked game in her expression, but she'd never let it control her. She was determined, strong. Stronger than he was. "Brolin might not have been able to describe the man who'd taken him, but we can trace the fingerprints back to where they originated. We'll find him—"

"I'm not going to lose you again!" The words left his mouth harsher than he'd meant. His ears rang as she flinched. He fought to breathe evenly, rage exploding through him. She wasn't the only one who had nightmares because of what happened on that cliff side. "I almost didn't make it in time when he took you. If I'd been one minute later…"

Braxton wouldn't play the what-if game. He shook his head to dislodge the memories. Reliving the past would only slow him down, consume him, and he'd lose the war before he had a chance to finish it.

"Do you really think I'd let him touch me again?" Liz locked onto his wrist and, faster than he thought possible, twisted his arm up and back. His childhood home blurred as she spun him head over heels. He hit the ground hard, the air crushed from his lungs. The chandelier above the entryway shook in the middle of the blackness closing in around the edges of his vision. He rolled onto his back, a groan escaping. *What had just happened?* She moved over him as pain radiated up his spine. His head throbbed, shoulders ached. Crouching beside him, she brushed his hair out of his face. "I didn't fight back when he put me in the trunk of his car because I want this baby more than anything, Braxton. I don't want to lose her. But don't mistake my decision for compliance. If he comes after me again, I will do what I have to, to survive."

She offered her hand, and he took it. Shoving to his feet, he ran his fingers through his hair to get it out of his face. "Where the hell did you learn to do that?"

"You're not the only one who's changed." Crossing her arms across her midsection, Liz shifted her weight against the mammoth wood banister lining the stairs. The sweats he'd dressed her in hung off her lean frame, but damn if she wasn't the epitome of everything he wanted. Everything he'd die to protect. "Let me guess. You were going to attempt to trace the feeds yourself from a laptop you stashed in your bag. Public place. Maybe a coffee shop close to the Anchorage police department that offers free Wi-Fi in case shots were fired."

Braxton slipped the backpack from his shoulder and set it on the floor. Rolling one shoulder back, he ignored the pain of landing on his own arm. "It crossed my mind."

"Except it won't work." She put one foot in front of the other, closing in on him slowly. Her mouth parted slightly, giving him flash-backs to the night they spent together, and his gut tightened in response. Liz dropped her voice. "You can try to convince yourself otherwise, but you need me in order to access Oversight."

Amusement hiked his eyebrows a little higher, his head still pounding from her little move that'd landed him on his back. "Wasn't hard to guess your password."

Just as it hadn't been hard for him to uncover her new name. He'd only had to think like her and home in on what she valued most in her life.

"But even you can't fake a retinal scan," she said.

Retinal scan? "I did not know you'd added that level of security."

"Give me the laptop." She stretched out her hand, a weak smile playing across her mouth.

"Vincent already forwarded the ballistics report on those bullets from the SUV. They're clean. So the shooter was sending me a message leaving the casings on the rooftop at the park. He wanted me to know this has to do with Justin Valentin. I'll dig into Agent Valentin's background, see if there's a connection there the NSA might've missed."

It was a start, and her plan wouldn't put her in immediate danger unless the shooter was monitoring Justin Valentin's records. Even then, Braxton's network rerouted his IP addresses all over the globe. The shooter would have a hard time nailing down their location for at least a couple of days. Braxton hefted his backpack up, handing it off to her. "And what am I supposed to do in this plan?"

She shouldered the pack and leveled her chin with the floor. Brilliant beams of light stretched through the wall of windows to his left, highlighting the spots of amber in her eyes. "You'll tell me you're going to stay."

His stomach dropped. Stay? That wasn't part of the deal. "It's not that easy—"

"Say those words, and I will do everything I can to make sure the NSA can't touch you." Stepping into him, she framed the side of his face with one hand. "I'll make sure you can come home. We can raise this baby. Together.

We can give her a family, and whether or not that includes your father is up to you."

"You don't know what you're asking, Liz." Air stuck in his throat. Curling his hands into fists, he put a few more inches of space between them. He slipped out of her reach, her eyebrows drawing together in confusion. "You need to know the truth before you ask something like that."

A half-hearted smile stretched across her mouth. "What are you talking about?"

"The reason I left four months ago." He stroked one hand down his beard. Hell, it wasn't supposed to be like this. She wasn't supposed to want him to stay, not when they both knew it couldn't last. Braxton dropped his hand to his side. "I'm the one who sold classified intel on Oversight."

Chapter Twelve

He'd…sold the intel on her program. "To the man trying to kill me and our baby?"

"Yes," he said. "The transaction was anonymous. I had no idea what he was going to do with the intel or that he'd come after you…"

His voice faded in her ears. Her knees shook as she stepped back. Despite the size of his childhood home, the entryway wasn't that big. There was only so far she could go and stay within reach of slapping him as hard as she could. "So all those interrogations the NSA put me through…when I told them you weren't the leak, I was committing treason."

Elizabeth ran a hand through her hair, fisting a tight knot between her fingers. No, no, no, no. None of this made sense.

"Everything that is happening is one hundred percent my fault, and you have my word I will never stop trying to make it up to you."

He took a step forward, but she countered almost instantly, and he froze, hands raised.

"You make it sound so easy." Think. Focus. No. Fury exploded from behind her sternum, and all rational thought disappeared. Elizabeth dropped the laptop bag and shoved at him with her unbroken hand as her lower lash line burned. "You put my life in danger." Pushing him again, she fought to keep the tears from falling. "You put our baby's life in danger."

The head wound, the bruised ribs, the broken wrist. She could take the physical injuries. But the emotional? She couldn't put a cast on that. Nausea rolled in her stomach. Oh, hell. Not now.

The three notches between his eyebrows deepened as Braxton dropped his hands to his side. He made another attempt to close in on her. "Sprink—"

"Don't call me that." She forced herself to breathe evenly around the bile working up her throat. Around another wave of betrayal. Around the stabbing pain in her chest. How could she have been so stupid? When Braxton had first informed her the feeds had been hijacked, she'd said it was impossible. Because it was. Less than a dozen government officials had clearance to know about the project. Without chalking it up to luck, a civilian wouldn't have been able to uncover her darkest secret. Unless someone handed them the information. She studied Braxton now and, for the first time, saw him for what he really was. "The intel you sold. It was how to hijack Oversight's feeds, wasn't it? Only in order take control of my program, you knew he needed me. That's why you came back. You realized the second you handed over that intel, he'd hunt me down."

"He already knew about the program. Knew exactly what he wanted and how to get it. I don't know how." Braxton nodded. "But when Dalton Meyer was killed, and the feeds were rerouted, I thought him coming after you next was a possibility."

"Why? Why would you do this to me?" She shook her head. "No. Don't answer that. I think I have a pretty good idea." Her hands shook at her sides. Elizabeth dug her toes into the hardwood to keep her balance, but her entire world had been upended. Slinging the bag over her shoulder once again, she maneuvered around him toward the front door. She didn't care she'd left her clothes and boots upstairs. She'd stop for supplies along the way. Reaching for the door, she turned her head enough to put him in her peripheral vision.

"When you realize the mistake you've made, don't try to find me. I don't *ever* want to see you again."

Shattering glass ripped her attention to the living room on her right. Then a hard *thunk* of metal against wood. An M84 grenade rolled toward her. Elizabeth caught only a glimpse of it before a wall of muscle crashed into her and pinned her against the floor. The oxygen knocked from her lungs as she covered her ears and closed her eyes. The thump of detonation reverberated through her. The backpack fell from her arm. Before she could take her next inhale, Braxton ripped her and the pack off the floor.

"Come on!" Smoke filled the room, stung her eyes as he led them toward the back of the house. "Cover your face with your shirt and keep your eyes closed. I won't let you go."

Another grenade broke through the window above the kitchen sink as they rushed through, and she didn't have enough hands to cover both ears without losing Braxton in the smoke. A white flash, an ear-deafening blast. Her ears rang, a high-pitched keen that worked to unbalance her and overwhelm her senses. Her shoulder hit the wall beside her, and she dropped Braxton's hand.

They were under attack. The shooter had found them. Found her.

His rough grip wrapped around her arms and thrust her forward. She jerked to the right into the downstairs office and dared to crack her eyes open. Smoke worked its way under the door, but not enough to sting.

Braxton pushed the black backpack toward her. She held on to it, heart pounding at the back of her head as he unzipped the bag and removed a gun. His lips moved. Nothing but muffled words reached through the ringing in her ears. He checked the gun's magazine, clicked off the safety and chambered a round. The movements were automatic, something he'd obviously worked at over the last few months.

She shook her head, pointing to her ear.

He took her hand then and mouthed, "I've got you."

A third percussion grenade shattered the office window as though the shooter were following them through the house from outside. She reached for Braxton, spinning them both inside the closet, and closed the door a split second before discharge. They had to get out of the house. Breathing ragged, head pounding, Elizabeth pushed out of the closet and went for the hallway.

Braxton's hand on her shoulder stopped her short of passing the large full bathroom on this level. She poked her head around the door frame from the hall. The bay window around the tub provided a perfect view into the spacious backyard.

And of the single masked man waiting for them outside.

Two taps on her shoulder spun her head around.

Braxton signaled them to the ground.

Getting to her hands and knees, she slipped past the bathroom, safeguarded by both walls that constructed the hallway. The garage was straight ahead, less than ten feet away. The backpack weighed her down and there was a chance they'd slip on the hardwood floors, but they didn't have a choice. They had to run for it.

Sliding against the wall, she sat back and closed her eyes, her hand across her lower abdominals. One breath. Two. They were going to make it out of this. She had to believe that. One tap on her arm brought her back into the moment. A combination of guilt and violence swirled in Braxton's gaze. He traced his fingers down one side of her face, and a shiver shook through her.

Elizabeth ripped away and pushed to her

feet. No. He should feel guilty. He was responsible for all of this. She pumped her legs fast, panting through her mouth. The strain at the back of her head increased. Her ribs protested, and her legs felt spongy and untrustworthy. Shattering glass and gunfire exploded from every direction the instant she left the cover of the hallway. She covered her head in a vain attempt to keep a bullet from turning her brain into mush and dropped, sliding into the garage door like an MLB player hitting home plate.

She didn't bother looking back for Braxton—he could take care of himself—and ripped the garage door open. She fell down the six concrete stairs into the garage. The door slammed shut on its own a moment later, Braxton crashing down beside her. Gunfire echoed from behind the thick steel as musty air worked its way into her system, but they couldn't stop now.

Braxton took her free hand again, helped her to her feet and pointed to the only window on the far wall of the garage. Wrenching out of his grip, she exhaled hard. It was their only escape. They wouldn't make it to the SUV parked outside. Not without putting themselves at the end of the shooter's barrel. He maneuvered her ahead of him. She climbed up the steel shelving, pulling off the pack in the process. Elizabeth shoved the bag through the window first as a loud bang erupted from inside the house.

The shooter had breached.

She pushed herself backward through the window, hung onto the ledge for a brief moment then dropped to the ground. The ringing in her ears subsided slightly. Thank heaven her pregnancy wasn't farther along. She might've never gotten through the window had the shooter come after her a few weeks from now. She got her bearings and listened for any sign she'd been seen.

Nothing.

Braxton dropped beside her, studying their new surroundings as she had. Without a fence separating the house from the woods, nothing could stop them from disappearing into the wilderness. Sirens echoed in the distance. Even a quarter mile away, one of the neighbors had most likely called police from the sound of the grenades.

The definitive sound of a chambering round swept a chill down her spine.

They weren't alone.

Her attention diverted to her right, toward the shadow at the corner of the garage, and

Elizabeth stepped back. How had he found them? Her stomach dropped. "Braxton…"

"Neither of you seem to understand." The shooter followed their every move as her bodyguard shifted in front of her. Dressed in a nicely pressed suit, ski mask included, the shooter obviously wasn't working for mobility, an advantage if things got physical. The ringing stopped in one of her ears, but the percussion grenade had knocked out her balance. She'd fight through it. Because there was no way in hell she'd let him take her again. The man who'd kidnapped her not forty-eight hours ago approached slowly, those black eyes sizing up Braxton from head to toe. Then raised his gun. "Elizabeth is coming with me."

He fired.

"No!" Liz's scream pierced through the pain-induced haze clouding his head. Blood slipped through his fingers as Braxton gripped his left thigh. The muscles in his leg strained as he kept himself from screaming. The bullet hadn't come out the back of his leg. Which meant there was a good chance it'd hit bone. Didn't matter. Liz mattered. Keeping her safe mattered. He focused on the feel of her fingernails digging into his shoulder to keep him upright, her mouth at his ear as the shooter closed in on his prey. Her. "Come on. Get up, damn it."

He shoved the pain to the back of his mind. The bastard wouldn't touch her. Not again.

"Get out of here, Liz." He shifted his weight onto his uninjured leg and took position in front of her. His jeans clung to him in spots where blood spread, but it wouldn't be enough to slow him down. This ended now. Right here, right now, this was where Liz's new life started. "And whatever happens, don't come back for me."

He didn't give her a chance to respond as he rushed toward the shooter. The bastard fired another shot, barely missing Braxton, and squeezed the trigger a third time. The bullet skimmed across his chest as Braxton turned to avoid the shot. Snow and ice worked into his boots, distracted him from the pain shooting up his leg. He collided with the shooter and tackled him to the ground. The gun disappeared into a snowdrift, out of sight.

The shooter slammed a knee directly into the right side of Braxton's jaw, but Braxton didn't loosen his grip around the operative's perfectly pressed suit. Braxton pulled his elbow back and slammed a fist into the shooter's face. Once. Twice. He pressed his knee into the shooter's sternum to keep him in place as he hit the shooter again and again. His heart threatened to beat out of his chest as the man beneath the ski mask blocked the next hit. With a kick to center mass, Braxton flew backward, his childhood home nothing but a blur as he landed in three inches of snow.

The shooter hauled himself to his feet, brushing snow from that damn suit. "I told you before, Levitt. You can't stop me. Elizabeth is going to pay for what she's done. One way or another. And you? You're just in my way."

Pain splintered down his sternum. Braxton bit down harder and shook the ice from his hair as he straightened. Blood dripped into the snow, into his boots. If he could still walk, he could still fight. And hell, he'd fight to the death for Elizabeth Dawson. In fact, there was nothing he wouldn't do for her. He'd already lost her once. He wouldn't lose her again. "Even with a bullet in my leg, you won't get to her."

"In my experience, the strongest always fall the hardest." An audible snap broke through the pounding of Braxton's heart behind his ears, and a glint of sunlight reflected off the switchblade in the shooter's hand. The masked man came directly at him.

Wrapping both hands around the shooter's wrist, Braxton twisted to one side to avoid being gutted right on his own front lawn. He hauled the SOB's wrist down over his knee—hard—and forced the shooter to drop the blade. Swinging himself around, he wrapped his forearm around the bastard's neck and squeezed. He locked his arm in place with his free hand, leveraging the shooter's head against his chest. Gloved hands fought to pry off Braxton's hold. In vain. But a swift hit of the shooter's elbow to his rib cage knocked the air from his lungs. The shooter wrenched free, gripped Braxton's throat and forced him to the ground.

The attacker wrenched Braxton's arm behind his back and applied pressure. Pain unlike anything Braxton had experienced exploded from his shoulder joint. "Look at her, Levitt."

Deep in the snow, his body temperature dropped, froze his muscles, anesthetized the bullet wound in his thigh, but he found the strength to lift his head. There, not twenty feet away, Liz searched through the snow. Presumably for the gun the shooter had dropped. Damn it. Why hadn't she listened to him? She should've run as far and as fast as she could. It would've been the only way to keep her safe. She wouldn't find the Glock. Not in time.

"I'm going to kill her after I get what I need from her, but first, I'm going to make her watch you die." Leaning into Braxton, the shooter intensified the pressure in his shoulder until a bone-crunching pop blacked out his vision. "You should've killed me when you had the chance."

A scream ripped from between his clenched teeth. He couldn't stop it. The operative had dislocated his shoulder and possibly torn one of the ligaments. The scream died to a groan after a few seconds, and Braxton fought to breathe through the tremors and the wave of dizziness rocking through him. He crushed his forehead against chunks of ice and snow beneath him to stay in the moment. "Touch her, and I'll kill you."

"Unfortunately for you, you're not going anywhere." The weight against his back disappeared. Snow crunched beneath footsteps, and Braxton shot his hand out to stop the shooter from reaching her and hauled him back. The man in the suit slammed into the ground, and Braxton pushed to his feet with his uninjured arm.

"You're not very good at listening." He circled around the bastard, his injured leg barely holding him up. A wave of dizziness distorted his vision. He was losing too much blood. His body had started going into shock. Soon he wouldn't be able to think. To breathe. His blood pressure would drop, and he wouldn't be able to stand. His words wheezed from his aching throat. He wrapped his free hand around the operative's throat and pulled the man in the mask against his chest for better grip. "I said you're not going to touch her."

Liz scrambled to her feet, empty-handed. Hair in disarray, her eyes red from the percussion grenade smoke, she only stared at him. Waiting.

Braxton could kill the shooter now. End this. But Liz had too many nightmares as it was. She didn't deserve to live with that for the rest of her life. He should incapacitate the SOB, tie him up and wait for Anchorage PD to arrive. Then extract himself from Liz's life once and for all. It was what she wanted. What he should've done in the first place. Snowflakes fell in a thin veil of white between them.

"Braxton, look out!" Liz's warning came too late.

Pure agony washed over him as a second blade buried deep in his gut. The shooter's gloved hand fell away. Braxton dropped his hold on the shooter's throat and stumbled back as the man in the mask rolled out of reach. Hell, he hadn't seen that coming.

Liz rushed forward from across the yard, eyes wide. Too far away. Snow kicked up around her as he collapsed to his knees. His heart pounded even louder behind his ears. He had to slow his pulse. Braxton swallowed to get rid of the muffled ringing in his ears. The faster his blood pumped, the faster he'd pass out. And that wasn't an option. Cold worked through his jeans. He placed his uninjured arm on the ground to keep from falling over. No. He wasn't going to die. Not until she was safe. He fought to stand but fell back as the muscles in his thigh finally gave out.

The shooter maneuvered into his vision. Headed straight for Liz.

"Liz." A growl reverberated through him as he climbed to his feet. His vision blurred again, only the spotting of red dots in the snow clear enough. He forced one foot in front of the other. Move. He had to get to her. Determination propelled him to his feet. No thought. Only her. His Elizabeth.

Sweat dripped into his eyes, but he had enough focus to keep her in sight. A glint of metal caught his attention at his feet. One of the shooter's blades. Sinking into the snow a second time, he wrapped his hand around the handle then used every last bit of strength he had left to stand. Two steps. Three. Pain and exhaustion drained from his muscles as he caught sight of Liz's wide, fearful gaze. She countered the shooter's steps as he closed in on her but wouldn't be able to outrun him. Not unless Braxton slowed him down.

That was all he had to do. Give her the chance to escape.

Police sirens echoed in the distance. Anchorage PD would take him in, the NSA would send an agent to the station claiming him in the interest of national security and he'd never see Liz again. Probably spend the rest of his days locked away inside some black site the government would deny existed if she ever came looking for him. But she would be safe.

And he could never hurt her again.

Reaching out for the shooter, Braxton clamped his hand on the bastard's shoulder, but he was caught off guard when his opponent spun in his grip. Braxton hiked the blade over his shoulder and thrust down with everything he had left. Only the blade never made contact.

Grip tight around Braxton's wrist, the man in the suit wrenched the knife to one side and forced him to drop it. "Don't worry, Levitt. I'm going to take real good care of her for you."

"No." The rush of adrenaline Braxton had been surviving off drained from his veins as blood pooled in his shirt and jeans. Pain flared up his uninjured arm, but he wouldn't back down. And he'd never give up. Not when it came to Liz.

"Let him go." The chambering of a round into a gun barrel claimed his attention. Over the shooter's shoulder, he spotted Liz as she widened her stance, both hands gripped around the shooter's gun. Chocolate-brown eyes shifted to him as the man in the suit dropped his hold. With hands above his head, the shooter turned toward her, and she followed every move. "I stopped Braxton from killing you the first time. I'm not going to make the same mistake twice."

Braxton stumbled back, hand over the stab wound in his side. Blood dripped onto the snow as sirens grew louder. It was over. The nightmare was over.

"Are you going to kill me in cold blood, too, Elizabeth? Just like you killed Justin Valentin or any number of other operatives with your program?" The SOB didn't give her a chance to answer, lunging straight at her.

"No!" Braxton rocketed to his feet. Darkness closed in around the edges of his vision, but he fought back with everything he had.

Liz pulled the trigger. Once. Twice. The gun never fired. Her mouth dropped open. She stumbled backward toward the tree line, caged by a line of pines, reaching for something to use as a weapon as the shooter closed in. "Braxton!"

There was too much distance between them. He couldn't get to her fast enough.

"That gun doesn't work." Wrapping his arms around her, the man in the suit hauled Liz off her feet and spun her around, her back to his chest. The shooter pulled a smaller gun from his ankle holster and aimed directly at Braxton. "But this one does."

Gunfire exploded in Braxton's ears—then pain—right before darkness closed in.

Chapter Thirteen

"Braxton!" Elizabeth couldn't take her eyes off him, off his lifeless body in the middle of ever-darkening red snow. No. He wasn't dead. It wasn't possible. Because the last words she'd spoken to him had been filled with hatred for what he'd done. She'd told him she never wanted to see him again, that he'd never get to meet his daughter. The shooter tightened his grip around her waist, hauling her into him. She pushed against his hands, but he didn't budge. "Get up! Please, get up."

Her throat burned. Eyes stung. He couldn't be dead.

"Save your energy, Elizabeth." The man in the suit pressed the gun's barrel against her temple. Police sirens drew closer, but the shooter barely seemed fazed. "You're going to need it before I'm through with you."

She clenched her teeth to fight the fresh rush of hot tears. No. Something inside her snapped. Adrenaline flooded through her system. Digging her bare heels into the snow, she wrenched out of the shooter's grip and shoved him back. He wouldn't take her again. He wouldn't win. Braxton couldn't protect her anymore. She had to protect herself. And their daughter.

"I don't want to shoot you, but I will." The shooter stalked toward her, gun still in hand.

"That's funny. I really want to shoot you." Elizabeth stepped back toward the pines to keep space between them, hands fanned out to her side. Pain shot through the back of her foot as she stepped on a medium-size tree branch that'd fallen near the tree line. Cold worked through her borrowed sweats as her attention flickered to Braxton, still unconscious twenty feet away. She'd trained to defend herself and she'd do just that. For him. No time to grieve. Time to survive. She wrapped her grip around the dead branch and swung as hard as she could. The wood reverberated through her hand at contact with the side of the shooter's head.

She didn't wait to see if he'd gotten up and pumped her legs hard. The police must be close. They had to be close.

A growl reached her ears, and she pushed herself harder. Puffs of crystallized air formed in front of her lips as she headed for the thick wilderness behind Braxton's childhood home. Tears froze in their tracks down her cheeks, the dropping temperatures working to slow her down. She was a runner, but exhaustion pulled her down. Barreling footsteps echoed from behind.

"Help!" She screamed as loud as she could, branches cutting the skin across her neck and face as she raced into the woods. It was the only place she could lose him. Her mouth dried, her breathing loud in the silent wilderness. Was that an Anchorage PD cruiser she'd just heard from behind?

The trees started to thin, the light brighter here. She didn't dare stop. Didn't dare look back. *Keep going. Get to the road. Survive.*

A wall of muscle slammed her into the icy dirt.

"You're faster than I gave you credit for." His lips pressed into her ear, his breath hot against her skin. A tremor raked across her chest, intensifying everything around her. The trees. The roots. He wrapped both gloved hands around one of her ankles and pulled. "You know, in a way, I've always admired you. Your determination. Your creative nature when it came to your work. Who else but you could've created a program like Oversight?"

Elizabeth dug her nails into the frozen ground. All too easily, she imagined her boss, Sullivan Bishop, having to come down to the morgue to identify her and Braxton's bodies. Not going to happen. She had to go back. She'd lost Braxton once. She couldn't do it again. He was a part of her. The good and the deceit. He was hers to protect now. He was the family her daughter deserved.

"You've chosen a really awkward time to hand out compliments." Clamping on to the nearest root, she heaved herself closer to the base of the large pine. The root broke away clean, and he dragged her backward. She couldn't think—couldn't breathe—but kicked at him as hard as she could.

A groan filled the clearing, his grip on her ankle loosening, but she sure as hell wouldn't ask her attacker if he was okay. She clawed across the foliage, jaw locked against the pain tearing through her. A *whooshing* sound reached her ears, and she exhaled hard, frozen tears stinging her cheeks. A car. She'd reached the next road over.

Elizabeth embedded her fingernails into the nearest tree and lifted herself to her feet. Run. No looking back. Just run. She stumbled forward, gaining strength with each step before she was finally able to pick up speed. Every muscle in her body screamed for release.

Another car drove past. Louder. Closer. Breathing became easier, but…slower. Something wet and sticky clung to her borrowed clothing. Sap? Taking refuge behind a large tree, she looked back over her shoulder. No movement. He hadn't followed her? Pain registered as she forced her heartbeat to slow. Not sap. She touched the spreading stain on her right side. Blood. When had that happened? She hadn't even felt an injury. She couldn't think about that right now. Braxton was bleeding out from at least two gunshots and a stab would. She'd run out of time. Deep breath. She could do this. Clamping her hand over her wound, she pushed forward. Couldn't stop. The shooter would catch up any minute. She had to flag down a car and circle back to Braxton—

The ground dropped out from under her feet. The world tilted on its axis as she rolled end over end. Branches and bushes scratched at her skin as blackness closed in at the edges of her vision. Sliding down the last few feet before the road, Elizabeth closed her eyes as the oxygen rushed from her lungs, unsure how long she lay there.

"Liz!" a male voice called.

She recognized that voice. A deep rumbling tore down the road, growing louder, and she forced her eyes open. "Sullivan?"

"I've got tracks!" Her boss's voice grew fainter, but she couldn't respond. Not without giving away her position to the shooter.

No. This wasn't the end. Not today. Another explosion of pain throttled through her as she flipped onto her side. Her team had come. She wasn't alone. They'd recover Braxton, and— She covered her mouth to prevent the scream in her throat from escaping. Save energy. Keep moving. "Any extra calories you can sacrifice would help a lot right now, baby girl."

Thick trees lining the road made it nearly impossible for her to spot movement. If the shooter had followed her, there were countless points where she could be walking straight into another ambush. She wouldn't be able to see him coming. Elizabeth ran a bloodied hand through her hair. She had to risk it. She had to get to Braxton. Had to get to her team.

Briars and weeds sliced into the bottoms of her feet, but she forced herself to keep moving. Anchorage PD wouldn't have been far behind Sullivan and the rest of the team. Somebody was getting Braxton the help he needed. She had to believe that. The alternative would rip her world apart, and she wasn't sure how much more she could take after what they'd been through the last five days. How much more heartache was she supposed to bear.

Swiping a hand beneath her runny nose, Elizabeth held her breath at the sound of a snapping twig. Her head pounded in rhythm to her racing heartbeat. She froze, only redirecting her gaze toward the tree line. He'd found her. Was hunting her. The weight of someone watching her—stalking her—pressurized the air in her lungs. Her fingertips tingled with the need to find a weapon. A shadow shifted to her left, and every ounce of willpower screamed for her to run. The tree line was the only way back to Braxton. If the shooter stood between her and getting to him...

"There's nowhere you can run, Elizabeth. Nowhere you can hide." That voice. She'd never be able to forget it, and she automatically dug her fingernails into the center of her palms. The shooter stepped from the tree line, gun in hand. The black ski mask shifted as he spoke. "Haven't I already proven how far I'm willing to go?"

"You can't get access to Oversight's programming, can you? Even after I gave you the password when you threatened to throw me over a cliff." Elizabeth straightened. He was right. She couldn't run. She couldn't hide. She'd have to finish this herself. She'd have to go through him. It was the only way to save Braxton. "That's why you haven't killed me yet."

Which meant he wouldn't kill her until she gave him the access.

"Seems you've implemented security measures even I can't get past." The man in the mask held the high ground. Any movement and he'd have the advantage. And the longer they stood here talking, the faster Braxton bled out.

"And you never will." Despite the failed mission that cost Agent Valentin his life, Oversight saved thousands of lives every day by predicting violence and threats. She'd always be proud of that, and she'd do what she had to, to protect it.

Silence stretched between them for the space of two breaths. Three. Time was slipping away too fast. Every beat of Braxton's heart endangered his life. They were wasting time. Wrapping one hand around his opposite wrist, gun pointed toward his toes, the shooter seemed more businessman than professional hit man. Maybe federal agent. "I'll make you a deal, Elizabeth. You give me what I want, and I guarantee your bodyguard lives."

"There's no way I would ever trust you." She wasn't stupid enough to believe he'd ever keep his end of a deal between them. But if she could get close enough to Braxton—ensure he was alive—she could shut down Oversight on her own and end this nightmare.

"Then the alternative is letting him bleed out, and I put a bullet in you now." The shooter raised the gun with one hand. Taking aim, he scrambled down the hill and closed the short distance between them. He fisted the ski mask with his free hand and tugged it over his head. Familiar dark eyes centered on her. "Do we have a deal?"

"You." Her knees shook as she stumbled back from the man in the suit. Shaking her head, she fought to keep her balance. "That's not possible. They said you were—"

"Dead?" Faster than she expected, the shooter slammed the butt of his gun into the side of her face, and Elizabeth dropped hard. Darkness closed in around the edges of her vision, but in the center, a ghost from the past still stared down at her. "Let's just say it didn't stick."

DEATH HAD TO be earned.

But Braxton wasn't willing to pay the price. Not until he recovered Liz.

A migraine pulsed behind his eyes. Three hundred stitches. Two bullet wounds. One stab wound to the rib cage. Two transfusions of blood. Hell of a way to die. But this wasn't over. Liz was missing. Vincent Kalani and Sullivan Bishop had tracked her path through the woods behind his childhood home to the road. As well as the shooter's. Then they'd simply disappeared. Spots of blood had stained the snow in her tracks. She'd been injured. According to the forensics expert, there'd been clear signs of a struggle, but no evidence of where the bastard had taken her.

He forced his legs over the edge of the hospital bed, and another wave of pain shot through him. Braxton gripped the sheets in his hand. He neutralized the groan working up his throat. Didn't matter how many bullets he'd taken or how much blood he'd lost, he was getting Liz back. And he'd kill anyone who tried to stop him.

The hairs on the back of his neck stood on end. Damn, he wasn't alone, and hadn't realized it until right this second. How much anesthesia had the doc given him?

"Look at you sacrificing yourself for others, Levitt." Elliot Dunham, Blackhawk Security's private investigator, propped his feet up on the edge of the bed and laced his fingers behind his head. "From what Liz told me about you, I didn't think you had it in you."

Hell. Of all the people on Liz's team to send, her boss sent this one. "Aren't you supposed to be babysitting?"

"Ah, yeah. About that…" Elliot planted the chair back onto the gleaming white tile and rested his elbows against his knees. Narrowing his gaze, the former con man cocked his head. "I kind of…lost your dad."

A laugh stretched the stitches down his side. Braxton highly doubted that. His old man had a way of disappearing at exactly the right time with exactly the right amount of cash he'd stolen from people's wallets. "You might want to cancel your credit cards. You're about to learn who Brolin Levitt really is."

Elliot patted his back jeans pockets, then his jacket. "Wow, he's good. Didn't feel a thing. I'm going to have to get him to show me some moves."

"Good luck finding him." He'd probably never see his father again. No loss there. Although Liz might have a hard time with the old man's disappearance. She'd kept tabs on the addict, made sure he had a place to sleep at night, food to eat. One day she'd understand how pointless all of that was. Brolin Levitt was a selfish son of a bitch. She'd be better off not knowing the real coward behind the drugs. Shoving off the bed, Braxton dropped onto the floor and shot his hands out for balance. He'd been brought in through the emergency room doors seven hours ago. Liz could be anywhere by now. If that SOB hadn't gotten to her first.

"If you're going after her, you're going to want to see this." Elliot reached for a file folder on the side table and tossed it onto the bed beside Braxton. "Did a little digging into the background of the CIA agent who was killed during the trial run for Liz's program. Justin Valentin."

"You don't have clearance for that intel." Anticipation flooded through him as Braxton reached for the file. A clean-cut photo of the agent had been paper-clipped in front of a military service record, driving record, residency proof and a whole lot more classified documentation Braxton had never seen before. Specific missions, confidential informants Agent Valentin kept. Even as an analyst, he would've had to get clearance or federal warrants for the paperwork in this file. "Where did you get all this?"

"You don't want to know." Elliot leaned in closer from his position in the chair, dropping his voice to a whisper. "It's blackmail. I have files on everyone I investigate. And some people I don't investigate, but that stays between us. Also, I can see straight through your—"

Braxton closed the file and reached for the opening in the back of the hospital gown. If there was another way to make patients more uncomfortable, he didn't know how it'd be possible. He searched the room. Where the hell were his clothes?

"The hospital staff had a hard time getting all the blood out of your clothes. You know, because there was…a lot. So they were incinerated. Good news, though—" Elliot hauled a duffel bag from beside his chair into his lap "—I brought you some of mine. Should fit. Had to guess your shoe size. Don't tell Vincent, but they're his." The private investigator tossed the bag at him, and Braxton was forced to release his clutch on the gown to catch it. Elliot guarded his eyes, chin to chest. "So Liz built a program for the NSA to spy on civilians, huh? I knew I liked her."

Digging into the duffel bag, Braxton pulled jeans, socks, boots and a long-sleeve shirt from the depths. He dressed fast. Every minute he wasted here, the higher the chance he'd never see her again. Hiking his foot to the edge of the bed, he suppressed a groan as he laced his borrowed boots. Pain was temporary. Losing Liz, that would be forever. "The program was designed to identify terrorists and criminals before crimes actually happened. It worked ninety-nine percent of the time, too. Oversight has saved thousands of lives."

"But the one percent got a CIA agent killed last year," Elliot said.

"That mission tore her apart. Valentin had disguised himself as part of the group he'd infiltrated, and Oversight hadn't been able to tell the difference because of a line of broken code. Liz blames herself for the mistake." Braxton studied the photo of Justin Valentin for the second time and narrowed in on the color of the agent's eyes. Ice blue. Not dark enough for the man in the mask. Justin Valentin wasn't their unsub and had only a wife and two young boys left behind. None of whom he considered a threat as he looked over their financials within the file. The shooter could be anyone, doing this for any reason, as far as Braxton knew. His shoulders deflated, the stitches protesting along his rib cage. They were back at square one.

Hell, all of this could've been prevented if he'd just stayed.

"So does someone else. Whoever is trying to kill her planted Agent Valentin's fingerprints on those casings from the rooftop shooting." Elliot leaned back in the chair. "They wanted her to know they knew she created Oversight and about the failed trial run."

The fingerprints. They were the only piece of evidence left behind in this investigation. He had to look at that report again. "Give me your phone."

The private investigator tossed him the device, and Braxton wasted no time logging in to his own email for the ballistics report Vincent had forwarded him less than twelve hours ago. Scrolling past the diagrams and countless pages of analysis, he focused on the latent fingerprints recovered from the casings. The shading was too light to have been pulled directly from wherever the prints originated. Elliot was right. They'd been planted on those casings and purposefully left at the scene. Which meant the shooter had pulled them from somewhere else using tape or another adhesive. Something Agent Valentin had to have in his possession and the bastard coming after Liz had gotten ahold of.

"What do you got?" Elliot stood, circling the bed.

"These prints are too light to have been taken directly off the source. They were transferred at least once more onto those casings."

Braxton zeroed in on a corner of one print and turned the phone on its side to zoom in on the area. A small, clearly defined arrow interrupted the impression at the edge of the print. He'd seen that exact shape, combined with a circle and two more arrows like it, before. On the Trident—Beretta's logo. "The prints were originally lifted off Justin Valentin's service weapon. A Beretta 92 FS, if I had to guess."

Elliot took the phone, studying the impressions on the screen. "The CIA's favored handgun for their field agents. Very nice. Good catch."

"Whoever wants Liz dead got ahold of a CIA agent's service weapon in the middle of Afghanistan. Can't be a long list." The shooter had made this personal by coming after her. He'd obviously been close to Valentin, blamed her for the agent's death. Why else plant those fingerprints? Why else play this mind game? Braxton rolled back his left shoulder where he'd taken the second bullet during the fight. He exhaled hard against the pain but rolled it back again. "Valentin didn't have a partner?"

"Not according to his records." Elliot reached for the file on the bed, thumbing through the pages. "The last time Justin Valentin was assigned a partner was…" The private investigator scoffed. "A year ago. The

agency suspected the partner had sold classified information to the Russians, but the agent
died in the line of duty before charges could
be brought up. That sucks."

Braxton straightened a bit more, his instincts on high alert. "What's the agent's
name?"

"Liam Waters." Elliot looked up from the
file. "Why? You know him?"

"No." He'd never heard that name before,
but it was the only lead they had, and his gut
screamed this would get him closer to Liz.
Hell, he should've fought harder. He should've
been a step ahead of the shooter who'd taken
her, but he'd been so caught up in…her, he
hadn't been able to think straight for days.
And it'd gotten her kidnapped. Again. Braxton stretched the stitches in his shoulder. He'd
tear this entire city to pieces to find her. And
kill anyone who got in his way. "How fast can
you get access to Waters's files?"

"An hour, tops." The private investigator
folded his arms across his chest, file still in
hand, and leveraged his weight against the
edge of the bed. Gray eyes, darker than Braxton's, narrowed on him. "What are you thinking?"

"Make it thirty minutes." He couldn't wait
that much longer. Not when Liz's life was

at risk. Braxton pulled the shoulder holster, complete with a smuggled handgun, from the duffel bag, and maneuvered into it slowly. Another round of pain lightninged through his injuries, but he pushed it to the back of his mind. Nothing would stop him from recovering Liz. And if the shooter turned out to be a dead man after all, he'd make damn sure the bastard never got up again. "I want to know if former agent Liam Waters is really dead."

Chapter Fourteen

A dull ache at the base of her skull beat through her in rhythm to her heart rate. Elizabeth cracked her eyes then closed them again against the brightness of a wall of active monitors in front of her. Blurry streaks cleared. The wide bay window had been covered with thick blankets. Blue light from the screens highlighted the three walls and large box near a door in her vision but nothing more. No other details. No telling where the shooter had taken her.

Not the shooter. He had a name. Former CIA agent Liam Waters.

And he blamed her for his partner's death.

"You're awake." Footsteps echoed off the worn hardwood flooring, growing closer. "I was beginning to think I'd hit you too hard."

Flashes of the woods, of Braxton facedown in the snow, crossed her mind, and Elizabeth fought to swallow around the tightness closing in. If Anchorage PD or her team hadn't made it to the scene in time... She pulled against the handcuffs behind her back and two more pairs around her ankles and the legs of the chair. She wasn't going anywhere. A rush of nausea forced bile into her throat. She licked at dry lips. "How long have I been out?"

"About eight hours." Waters maneuvered into her vision and stood in front of her, gun loose in his grip at one side. Lines furrowed between his thick eyebrows, a head of dark hair wilder than she remembered from his files. Before he'd joined the CIA, Liam Waters had been part of the fleet antiterrorism security team, or FAST, where he'd been partnered with Agent Justin Valentin for a number of years then accused of selling classified intel to a Russian contact. After Oversight had misidentified Valentin for an extremist, she'd hacked into the agent's files. Wanted to know the man her program had killed. Agent Liam Waters had been in those files. As were the charges the CIA planned to bring against Agent Valentin's partner before Waters had been killed in action. Bruising shadows shifted in the light of the monitors as he spoke and, suddenly, he seemed so much... older than she remembered from his files.

Worn. Desperate. Not dead after all. "Recognize what's on the monitors?"

Elizabeth shifted her focus to the screens. City names from across the country popped up on the bottom of each monitor as it scrolled from image to image. Cars passed beneath cameras, civilians walked down streets, thin white squares homed in on, processed and identified facial features. The weight of Waters's attention settled on her. "You're the one who hijacked Oversight's feeds."

"And you're the one who killed my partner with it." Cords looped circles behind Waters's feet. Hundreds of them, all connected to the monitors, disappeared behind the door to her left. Not an exit. Most likely a server room, which meant the only way to escape was behind her. Waters crouched in front of her, his knees popping with the movement, gun still in hand. "Justin Valentin had a family. A wife, two boys. I showed up at his house every morning to pick him up for work for four years, and when their youngest was diagnosed with leukemia and they couldn't pay for the treatments, I did what I had to do to make sure they could. Of course, they'd known what I'd done. There was no hiding the fact I'd started selling intelligence to the Russians from my own partner. He was a good agent, but, as it turned out, a father would do anything to save his son. Justin helped me plan my own death. Because you see, they were my family, too." Waters stood, fanning his grip over the gun's handle. The monitors cast his features into shadow from behind. "Now those boys can't look at me without thinking of their dead father. His wife refuses to see me, won't take my calls. You did that. You took my family from me."

"I'm sorry." She forced herself to breathe evenly. Every moment of that failed trial had been burned into her memory. Braxton running to her cubicle with news of the mission go-ahead from her project supervisor, Dalton Meyer, her trying to shut Oversight down remotely. Nothing had worked. In the end, she'd been restrained by security and sealed in an office while the NSA had taken control of her program. She'd only learned of Oversight's mistake after the fact. And had taken the blame for it all. "I tried to stop them. I told them the program wasn't ready, but Meyer wouldn't listen—"

"You think I did all of this for an apology?" A low, dark laugh rumbled from deep in his chest, and a shiver shot across Elizabeth's shoulders. She interlaced her fingers tighter as he closed the short distance between them, her wrists straining against the handcuffs. He leveraged his weight against the back of the chair with one arm. A combination of spicy aftershave and sweat dived into her lungs. "No, Elizabeth. I brought you here so you can watch your creation burn. Then I'm going to kill you."

Shock rocked through her. Her mouth dried. She searched for something—anything—that would get her out of these cuffs. A paper clip. A nail. Maybe if she vaulted herself backward, the wood chair would break enough for her to get free. She was on her own. No matter how many times he'd been there before, Braxton couldn't save her now. "You can't shut the program down. Oversight made a mistake— *I* made a mistake—but it has saved countless lives over the past year. It's protected this country, stopped terrorists. Just as you have."

"And how many more families will be destroyed—families like Justin's—because of your mistakes?" Waters wrapped gloved hands around the back of the chair and shoved her forward until her knees hit the desk. The former agent gripped the back of her neck tight and thrust her over the keyboard. "You built the security for Oversight. You're going to tear it down."

Elizabeth clenched her teeth against the

stiffness in her neck. She pushed back, but Waters was so much stronger. And not handcuffed to a chair. A rush of dizziness distorted her vision. No, no, no, no. Not now. The sinking sensation that accompanied her blood sugar crashing pulled her farther into the chair. She fought to breathe through the disorientation. Didn't work. Nothing but food would combat the crash. Closing her eyes against the sudden brightness of the monitors, she dropped her head. And saw blood. The injury from the woods. Her blood pressure spiked. "My side is bleeding. My blood sugar is crashing. I need to eat. I'm no good to you in shock."

He dropped his grip on her neck and instead replaced it by pointing the gun at her left temple. He pressed so hard the steel cut into her skin, but she wouldn't disable the program. Not when the safety of an entire country had been put on the line. "Surprise me."

She bit her lower lip to distract herself from the crushing weight behind her sternum and the pain in her ribs. Nobody was coming to save her. She had to save herself. But she couldn't even do that if she was cuffed to this damn chair. Her senses had started adjusting to the surrounding darkness. There had to be something in this room she could use as a weapon. "If you want me to shut down the program, you're going to have to uncuff me."

"I've read your file, Elizabeth. I've watched you for months." He centered her in front of the nearest monitor. "I know what you can do with your hands. You tell me the second password, and I'll enter it."

He wanted to do this the hard way? Fine. "I told you before when you were threatening to throw me over a cliff. Even if you enter the password, there isn't only one level of security. Oversight doesn't work like that. I made sure no one person could take control of the system. So unless you have a retinal scanner in this dump, you're not getting into my program."

"Then I have no use for you." His rough exhale hit her collarbones as Waters compressed the gun's safety button off. "Blackmailing your bodyguard to get the intel I needed on Oversight was worth less trouble than you are. I'm done with you."

Blackmail?

"You don't have to do this. Justin wouldn't want this. His wife and those boys wouldn't want this." This wasn't how she'd die. Not after everything she'd been through the last five days. Not after losing the only man she'd ever wanted to spend the rest of her life with, the man who'd never get to meet his daughter. Her eyes burned. From the moment Braxton had shaken her hand at their first meeting to the moment he'd sacrificed himself for her to get away in his own front yard, he'd protected her. He'd stood by her side. He'd given her a glimpse of the family she'd always wanted. Needed.

"Guess we'll never know, will we?" he asked.

Elizabeth licked at her lips one more time. She might've already lost Braxton. She wasn't about to lose their baby. "Please, I'm pregnant."

The gun faltered in Waters's hand. "That's not possible. I've been following you for months. I've read your medical records."

"Then you suck at your job. Otherwise you would've noticed me walking into my doctor's office last week." She scanned the room a second time, locking on a blue-and-white pen on the floor to her right. She could do a lot of damage with a pen, but getting her hands on it was a different skill set entirely. Pressing her toes into the floor, she tipped the chair's front legs back a few centimeters at most. She didn't dare look at Waters's face. Any sudden movement on her part could force him to pull the trigger. But if she could walk out of this unscathed, she'd take the risk. "You hijacked the feeds to an all-seeing program. Review the records again. I'm sure they're updated by now."

"You're lying." Keeping the gun aimed at her head, the former agent rounded into her vision. Bruising darkened the shadows beneath his eyes where she'd clocked him with the handle of his gun on Seward Highway, and a small bit of her hoped it hurt like hell. But then those dark eyes centered on her, and everything inside her went cold. "At this point, Elizabeth, I think you'll say anything to stay alive, but you can't get out of this. You're going to die today."

"No, I'm not." She kicked against the floor, every muscle in her body going rigid as the chair tipped backward. The room blurred a split second before she hit the hardwood. Cracking wood claimed her attention, but not for long. Pain stretched up her crushed arms as she rolled from the debris, her wrists still cuffed. She wrapped her fingers around the pen and pushed the sharp end into the keyhole. Slim chance this would work, but she wouldn't go down without a fight. For Braxton. For her baby.

"Clever." Liam Waters stood over her, gun raised. Slipping his finger over the trigger, he widened his stance. "But, tell me, honestly, how far did you think you could run this time?"

"Who said I'd try to run?" The cuff loosened from around her casted wrist, and Elizabeth shot her foot upward. Connecting with Waters's gun, she sent it flying across the room. The gun discharged, the bullet arching wide, forcing her to cover her head with her arms in an empty attempt to avoid being shot.

With her next breath, Waters straddled her midsection and crushed the oxygen from her lungs. He pinned her against the floor. "Why won't you just die?"

The door behind her slammed open. "Get your damn hands off of her."

BRAXTON FLEW OVER LIZ, tackling the former CIA operative to the floor. Monitors on the desk shook from the quake then toppled face-first around them as he pulled his elbow back. Glass and metal hit the hardwood, but nothing would distract him from finishing the job. Not this time.

"How many times do I have to kill you before it sticks?" Waters slammed an elbow into his face and twisted out of Braxton's reach.

Shooting his hand out, Braxton caught the edge of the shooter's suit jacket, but not enough to pull the bastard back. The sound of tearing fabric drowned the pounding of his pulse behind his ears. Waters went for one of the largest monitors, hauling it over his head.

Every stitch in his body protested as Braxton rolled out of the way and shot to his feet. He grabbed Waters by the arm and whirled him into the nearest wall. Adrenaline sang through his veins, blocking out the pain of his injuries. It wouldn't last long, but he'd sure as hell make the most of it. Shifting his weight back as Waters swung a right hook, Braxton kicked out the operative's knee and followed it up with a punch to the gut. "No one hurts my family and gets away with it."

Waters stared up at him. Blood dripped from the former agent's lip. Swiping it off with the back of his hand, the SOB cracked a smile. Then Waters swung up. Flesh met bone and Braxton spun backward, barely catching a glimpse of Liz as she worked to free herself from three different sets of cuffs. He landed face-first against the floor. Footsteps echoed off the hardwood. "Funny. I was thinking the exact same thing."

Liz's gaze shot up, widened at the sight of Waters closing in, then homed in on the gun against the far wall. Braxton could tell from the determination in her eyes she was going to make a run for it.

Waters lunged as Liz pushed off the floor. He got there first, wrapping his hand around the gun and swinging it wide toward her. Braxton launched to his feet, but not before Liz caught Waters's wrist in one hand and pushed her casted hand up under his jawline. Shoving him back, she wedged the former agent between herself and the wall, but there was nowhere else to go.

"Liz!" Braxton took a step forward then collapsed to one knee. The stitches in his thigh had torn. Blood seeped through his jeans. Damn it.

She let go of the former agent's throat then slammed her cast against the gun, dislodging Waters's hold on the Glock. And hell if that wasn't the sexiest thing he'd ever seen. But Liz wasn't fast enough. With one blow to the face, she went down. She hit the ground hard, a groan filling his ears, and nothing but rage consumed him.

Braxton closed the space between him and Waters in two steps and lunged feet first. His boots connected with the shooter's sternum, and they collapsed to the floor. Air stuck in his lungs, but he barely had time to stand before Waters came around. Braxton stumbled, shooting his hand out toward the dropped gun. The metal slipped against his palm. He tightened his grip and swung the gun around.

But Waters had the bigger card to play.

With a simple white-and-blue pen.

Crouching over Liz, the operative held the pen to her jugular, waiting for Braxton to make his next move. Waters's shoulders rose and fell in rapid succession in rhythm to his strained breathing. If Braxton had to guess, the operative had broken a rib or two, but he hadn't let it slow him down. It'd take more than a few broken bones to finish this. "I've spent the last year waiting for this moment. You're not going to stop me from getting my partner's family the justice they deserve, Levitt."

Blood spread through his T-shirt, soaking the waistband of his jeans, but Braxton pushed the distraction to the back of his mind. Hell, he'd tear every stitch a hundred times if it meant protecting the woman he loved. Screw the pain. Screw the NSA. He'd left Liz behind once. He wouldn't make the same mistake again. He wasn't going anywhere. Not without her. Lifting the gun, he centered the former CIA operative in his sights. Liz had stopped him from killing the bastard once, and it'd been a mistake. "It's over, Waters. Liz is mine. And I don't share."

Swaying, the former agent dropped his chin but only fanned his fingers around the pen. "I should've killed you four months ago when I had the chance."

"Yeah." Braxton held the gun steady, ready for the last round. Liam Waters wasn't leaving this room alive. Killers like him didn't give up easily. The former CIA agent would keep coming after her. And Liz—and their baby— deserved a life better than one on the run. He could give them that. "You should have. But if you make another move, I'll make damn sure you never get back up."

"Let's see who's faster." Waters raised his hand, ready to plunge the pen into Liz's throat as she lay unconscious, and Braxton pulled the trigger. One bullet ripped through the operative's shoulder but didn't bring Waters down. He fired again, the gun kicking back in his hand. The second shot hit center mass. The shooter held his arm up but dropped the pen. Collapsing to the floor, Liam Waters stared at the peeling yellow ceiling, one hand pressed against the wound beneath his sternum.

"I feel like you should've known not to bring a pen to a gunfight." Braxton approached slowly, heart threatening to break apart his rib cage. He kicked the pen out of Waters's reach as the shooter dived into unconsciousness, head slumping to the side. The operative's chest stilled, one last exhale reaching Braxton's ears.

Liam Waters was dead.

Dropping to his knees, he framed Liz's face with one hand, sliding the pad of his thumb across her bottom lip. "Liz."

Her resulting groan set every cell in his body on fire. She swung her head toward him and cracked her eyelids. Deep brown eyes locked on him, and his world shattered. Hell, they'd survived. Together. The nightmare was over. And they—relief coursed through him—they could get their lives back. They could start their family. If she'd have him. Brushing her hair behind her ear, he studied her for any other injuries. "Can you move?"

"My blood sugar…" Her hands shook as she wrapped them around the back of his neck. "I haven't eaten."

"Here." He set the Glock on the floor then reached into his back pocket and pulled out two granola bars. Unwrapping both, he dumped the broken pieces into his palm and lifted her against him. "It's not much, but I brought something in case you crashed again."

She closed her eyes, chewing methodically, and sank against him. "You really know the way to a woman's heart."

"Just yours." A smile pulled at one corner of his mouth. He held on to her, resting his cheek against the top of her head. A combination of lavender and chocolate overwhelmed his senses, and he breathed in as much as he could. "I got you. You're safe now."

A gunshot exploded in his left ear.

Liz arched against him, mouth open, eyes wide, but her gasp said it all.

She'd been hit.

Tearing her away from him, Braxton spun. He reached for the gun in Waters's hand. The bastard wasn't dead yet, barely keeping himself upright. Braxton wrapped his fingers around the barrel and wrenched it from the SOB's grip, turning the gun on the shooter. Braxton pulled the trigger. One shot. Waters's head snapped back, a bullet between the eyes. The body dropped hard. And the threat was neutralized.

A sharp inhale brought him back into the present. Braxton lunged. On her stomach, sprawled across the hardwood, Liz didn't move. He reached for her, lifted her upper body into his lap. The bullet hadn't come out her chest. The damn thing was still inside her. No. He would not lose her. Not after everything they'd been through.

"It burns." A tear streaked down the side of

her face into her hairline. Her throat worked to swallow as blood rushed over his fingers. She fought to speak, licking her lips, her gaze heavier than he'd ever seen before. Streaks of blood coated her tongue. Hell, the bullet had punctured one of her lungs. Her breath shortened. "Braxton…"

"I've got you, Sprinkles. Stay still. I'm not going to lose you again. I'm never leaving you again." The peeling walls blurred in his vision as Braxton hoisted her into his arms and encased her against him. He carried her out of the room as fast as he could. Footsteps echoed up the second level as Vincent and Elliot raced to intercept. He'd had the private investigator inform the rest of the Blackhawk Security team about this property owned under one of Waters's aliases before Braxton had raced from the hospital. He owed them his life. Stairs jostled their descent, and he tightened his hold on her to keep the slug from shifting deeper. The bullet was too close to her spine. He nodded back toward the room upstairs to direct the team to Waters's body, his focus entirely on the woman in his arms. The love of his life. The mother of his child. Neither Vincent nor Elliot bothered examining the crime scene. Instead, they followed Braxton downstairs to the waiting ambulance.

"Stay awake, baby. I have more granola bars where these came from. And there might even be some ice cream and rainbow-colored sprinkles left over for you. But you've got to stay awake, okay?"

"There sure as hell…better be." Liz went slack in his arms as she gave in to unconsciousness.

Chapter Fifteen

Searing heat enveloped her scalp as Elizabeth held herself under the shower spray. Her tailbone had been bruised, if not cracked. The laceration in her ribs from the woods was almost too much to bear. Luckily, surgeons had been able to remove the bullet from her back and patch her lung. But, hell, it felt good to be in her own house. She didn't even want to look at the rest of her body. She washed two-day hospital grunge off, the simple idea of soap helping her muscles relax. As did the gun sitting on the small bathroom sink to her right. Cold air rushed against her as she stepped from the shower and tied a towel around herself.

She didn't have to turn around to know Braxton had let himself in. The weight of his attention from the doorway pimpled goose bumps across her back. "How are you feeling?"

"Still hurts to breathe, but I'm alive." Two

days. Two days since he'd charged through that door and shot the man determined to destroy her life. Two days since she'd woken up, facedown on a stretcher getting wheeled into surgery with him by her side. He'd promised never to leave her again, but the situation between them hadn't changed. He'd sold classified intel to an enemy combatant, and the NSA would charge him with treason the second they got their hands on him. So what were they supposed to do now? "Thanks to you."

Liam Waters's body had been recovered by Anchorage PD, as had mountains of evidence proving he'd been stalking her for months. He'd been careful, planned every step and stayed ahead of her the entire time, but even knowing the former agent would never come after her again, she couldn't relax.

"You did a damn good job protecting yourself, Sprinkles." Braxton crossed his arms over his torso, all three hundred stitches securely in place again. "Have you slept?"

"No." The memories running through her head wouldn't let her. It'd take time for her to scrub the slate clean. She reached for the gun on the sink.

Braxton struggled to straighten, the pain in his expression evident. She wasn't the only one who'd been through hell over the last week. "Liz—"

"Waters told me why you did it." She fisted the towel tighter. Waters had blackmailed him. She didn't know all the details, but if Braxton had proven anything over the last week, it was that he'd do anything to protect her. And he'd left thinking the former CIA agent would leave her alone after he'd delivered the intel. But killers rarely kept their end of the deals they struck. She'd learned that the hard way. "He threatened to kill me unless you got him the intel on Oversight, right? Why didn't you tell me?"

"Any reason I gave after you found out would look like a desperate attempt to win you back." The vulnerability and sorrow in his voice raised her body's awareness of him to new heights. "I needed you to find out on your own."

Elizabeth gripped the weapon harder, hot tears in her eyes. "And if he'd never told me, you were willing to walk away from us forever? Never meet your daughter?"

"If it kept you alive, yes." The solemn expression etched onto his face penetrated deep into her soul, as though he'd stolen the very oxygen she needed to live. "I told Waters how to access Oversight's feeds, and people died because of it. Because of me. I'll never be able to forgive myself, and I'll understand if you can't, either. But I made you a promise. I'm not leaving you behind. Not again. I'll avoid arrest as long as I can to stay in Anchorage. For you."

The guilt she'd witnessed inside Braxton consumed his irises. The shock of his admission cut her like a blunt blade, rough and painful. Dalton Meyer and Liam Waters had been killed, an entire country had been put at risk, all because Braxton had tried to protect her.

"You gave up classified intel to a former CIA agent then came back to stop him when you realized that he was going to use it to hunt me down." She could barely believe the words coming from her own mouth.

"He threatened to kill you. I may have lost my temper." He stepped forward, slowly closing the space between them. The steam from the shower penetrated through the thick towel wrapped around her. Or was it her heart racing out of control? He glanced at the gun in her hand. "You don't need the gun, Liz. Not for me."

Silence reigned, perfect silence almost too good to be true.

It took three deep inhales before she could look at him again. Liam Waters would've gotten his hands on Oversight's intel one way or another, maybe tortured and killed dozens more people to do it. She knew that now. There was no reasoning with him, no convincing him killing her wouldn't bring his partner back. And she and Braxton had stopped him. The man standing two feet from her had ensured the world had one less killer to worry about.

Her body ached as Elizabeth set the gun back on the sink. The internal torture he'd put himself through showed in his expression, and she reached for him, framing the side of his jaw with her uninjured hand. His warmth burned a hole through the last bricks of the wall she'd created around her heart, desolating everything she'd held against him.

He'd done it all for her.

"The gun's not for you. I just…need it for a little while longer. What you did, it made me feel protected." She swiped her thumb beneath one bright green eye. Careful to avoid the bandages over his left shoulder, she stepped into the comfort of his arms. How could she ever have thought he'd betray her? The past week alone was proof enough. He'd do anything to protect her and their baby. And she'd do anything to keep him in her life. "Made me feel loved."

"You're safe now. It's over." He ran his fingertips through her hair. The slight tremble against her scalp mimicked the uneven thump of her pulse. Elizabeth caught the struggle to fill his lungs but couldn't force herself to straighten. Not yet. She hadn't felt so content in months, his skin warm, traces of his clean, masculine scent diving deep into her pores. Her nerves settled the longer she counted his heartbeat. "I won't let anyone hurt you ever again."

"I know," she said.

Physical tension drained from him. Only the sound of their combined heartbeats filled her ears, but her fingers tingled with the urge to touch him. Elizabeth slid her hand across his torso, following the peaks and valleys created just for her. The soul-deep craving she'd always had for him erupted as she craned her head up. The emptiness in those irises had vanished, leaving nothing but her reflection in his gaze.

"I was going to stock your freezer for you." Braxton swiped a strand of hair behind her ear, sending liquid pleasure shooting to her core. His laugh vibrated through her. "Then realized you already have three gallons of chocolate ice cream."

"I stopped at the store right after they released me from the hospital." Something stirred in her lower abdominals. If she was honest with herself, she'd already made her decision, but so much had happened between them. He'd sold classified intel to save her life, had gone as far as putting his own life in danger for her, but the sting of his disappearance hadn't lessened. Four months of wondering, of questions, had nearly driven her to the point of insanity. She couldn't go through that again. "I was hoping we might be able to share a bowl tonight. And every night after that."

Disappointment overwhelmed his features, and her heart shattered from the agony consuming him. She'd experienced the same pain when Braxton had vanished and had completely lost herself inside that betrayal. "I can't. Not without dragging you and the baby into the NSA's manhunt for me. I'll stay in Anchorage, but it'll be at a distance."

Stepping back, Elizabeth ran the pad of her thumb over his left cheekbone. He lifted his gaze to her, staring at her as though she was the center of his entire world. Just as he had when they'd first met. She'd never get used to that. "And if I told you the NSA didn't get to decide our future?"

Those mesmerizing green eyes narrowed on her. "What do you mean?"

"Answer the question." Elizabeth pulled back, eager for his response. This was the defining moment, the chance to risk it all. And if he didn't take it? Her insides churned at the thought. But she'd move on. She'd raise this baby alone. She'd tell her daughter the truth. That her father had to stay in hiding to protect them. "Would you stay here with me—with us—and give us another shot if the manhunt was called off?"

"Damn right I would." Braxton threaded his fingers through the hair at the back of her neck, molding her to him. "Making you mine is the only thing I've wanted since you walked into the office all those years ago."

Her cell phone dinged with an incoming message from the other room. Perfect timing. "Good. I called Dalton Meyer's replacement when I got home from the hospital and told them I would only help restore Oversight's feeds for the NSA if they cleared the charges against you."

Braxton's expression slackened. He tried to pull away, but she secured him against her. No. No more running. No more lies. From now on, they'd be honest with each other. "Liz, you didn't have to do that. I would've figured something out—"

"Yes, I did. You saved my life more times

than I can count. It was time to return the favor." She'd vowed never to work for the NSA or touch Oversight's programming again but ensuring Braxton could help raise their daughter, that he could make them a family, was worth it. "As twisted as it sounds, Waters died for the one person who mattered most to him in the world. His partner. I realized when he had that gun to my head, if I had to, I would do the same thing for my partner." Fisting her fingers in his T-shirt, she pushed against him slightly. "I love you. I never stopped loving you, and I want you here. I want you to help me raise this baby. I want to be a family."

"I love you, too." His breath warmed her neck. Pressing himself against her, he smoothed the tip of his nose along the outside cartilage of her ear. A shudder ran across her collarbones and down her spine, and she closed her eyes to heighten her senses. "What do you say we get out of here? You, me, no more secrets, no guns. Just the open ocean and sandy beaches for a few weeks."

After what they'd been through, she needed it. She spun in his arms, securing the towel around her once again, and wiped steam from the mirror. She'd have to clear the time off with Sullivan and the rest of the team, but she doubted Blackhawk Security needed her for the next month or so. "I'm bringing my gun."

"You say the sexiest things." Braxton slid one hand along her thigh, below the hem of the towel. The rough patches on his fingertips scraped against her skin, but not uncomfortably. He buried his lips in the crook between her neck and shoulder. He planted a kiss against her skin, tracing the edge of her tendon with his lips. She grew painfully aware of the reaction his lips elicited in her lower abdominals. He slid his hand over their baby from behind, lowered his chin onto her shoulder and held her against him. "Marry me."

Interrupting her next inhale, he guided her head toward him and crushed his mouth against hers, urgent, warm. Her vision wavered as she surrendered herself over to him completely. After almost four months of missing his touch, she couldn't think of anything but the towel and his clothes separating them. Their injuries wouldn't allow them to fulfill all of their physical desires, but having him close was more than enough. Pulling away for a moment, her lips growing cold without his, she reveled in the weight lifting from her chest. He was a free man. He was hers. "Deal."

Hints of that gut-wrenching smile pulled at

one corner of his mouth, and her pulse rocketed higher. He swept a stray piece of soaked hair off her face then brought her hips into the circle of his arms. "I only have one condition."

"You realize you're the one who proposed to me, right? I'm supposed to make the conditions." She melted from the warmth radiating from under his clothing. Something exploded inside, seared her from the inside out and destroyed the horror-filled memories of the last week. Her heart thundered with a renewed possibility of finally having the man she'd wanted from the start, of starting their family together, and she smiled against his lips. "But go ahead. Name your price."

"We get on a plane tomorrow," he said. "And you marry me by sunset."

"What are we supposed to do until then?" Elizabeth had meant the question innocently enough, but the desire burning in Braxton's gaze filled her thoughts with plenty of things they might be able to do despite the near-death injuries they'd sustained.

"I have a few ideas." Braxton pulled her closer, her back pressed to his front, and fit her against him. His pulse was slow and steady between her shoulder blades, and she collapsed her head back against his shoulder. "One of them involves getting this towel off you."

She wrapped her hands around the Glock on the counter and dropped it to her side. Safety on. She might need the extra security for a few more weeks, until the nightmares subsided for good, but at least she'd have Braxton at her side to help her forget. Forever. "Good luck with that."

Five months later...

SCREAMING. BLOOD. ICE CHIPS. More screaming. All for the tiny, perfect human in his arms.

"Karina Dawson-Levitt." He couldn't believe it. Braxton cradled his daughter tighter. Mere hours ago, they'd rushed to the hospital, and before he knew it, here she was. Their baby girl opened her mouth wide in a yawn, and his eyes burned. Hell, he'd never been so happy in his life. A laugh rumbled through him. "Welcome to the world, half-pint."

"Hey, I pushed that watermelon out. I get to hold her, too, you know." Liz slid her fingers across his arm, pulling him back toward her on the bed. The damn thing wasn't wide enough for all three of them, but there was no way he was moving from this spot. Liz pressed against him on his right, baby Karina in his arms. His wife rested her head on his shoulder and set her hand over his heart, right where it belonged. A moan filled his ears as she glanced up at him. "She's so perfect, I want to eat her up. Want to count her fingers and toes again?"

"No, let's let her rest. She's got to save her energy so she can keep us up all night." Planting a kiss in Liz's hair, Braxton caught movement through the small window in the hospital room door. They'd held them off as long as they could, but the team had gotten restless. There was no stopping it, but he was determined to stretch out this moment of peace as long as he could. Stroking his fingers over Karina's baby-soft skin, he braced himself against the oncoming chaos. "They're going to break down the door if we keep them waiting any longer."

"You can let them in in a minute. But only because I'm afraid Elliot will start telling the staff he's a doctor to get in here." Liz leveraged her hands into the mattress and straightened, then ran her hands through her hair. "Hell, he probably has the credentials already made just in case."

"You look beautiful." Braxton brushed a stray piece of hair behind her ear, sliding his thumb across her bottom lip. "You grew a human inside your body. What you did was amazing, and you're more beautiful now than ever."

He still couldn't believe she'd married him on that beach, couldn't believe she'd chosen him after he'd failed to keep her safe. With her work for the NSA behind her, Oversight up and running, and the charges dropped against him, he'd spent the last five months making it up to her every way he knew how. And he'd keep trying for the rest of his life. Without her... No. He wouldn't think of a life without her. There was no life without her. She'd been the one to get him through the darkness. Everything he wanted was right here in this room. And he'd fight like hell to keep it that way.

The CIA had taken possession of Liam Waters's body after the fight in his hideout. The bastard would never hurt her again. Only after receiving confirmation his remains had been incinerated had her nightmares finally subsided. She didn't need to sleep with the gun stashed under her pillow at night. She was safe. And the past was officially dead.

She leaned into his palm, kissing the callused skin there with a wide smile. Her breath brushed lightly over his wrist, and every nerve ending in his body went haywire. For her. "You're just saying that so I'll let you eat the cookies the nurses brought me to get my blood sugar back up."

"I love you." Braxton kissed her with everything he had then handed off the tiny human to her mother. He maneuvered off the bed and crossed the room. Spinning back toward her before he opened the door, he pointed at her. "But I'm getting those cookies one way or another."

He wrenched the heavy metal door toward him, and in three breaths her team flooded the room with congratulations. Sullivan Bishop, Elliot Dunham, Vincent Kalani, Anthony Harris and Glennon Chase all closed in on his wife and daughter. The only operative missing was Kate Monroe, but he was sure the profiler would get to meet the newest member of the Blackhawk Security team soon.

Liz's smile brightened despite the grueling process she'd gone through to deliver their baby, and a rush of joy had him cracking his own smile.

That was his wife. His daughter. His life.

Braxton saw the future in that moment.

And, damn, it looked good.

* * * * *

Read on for a look at the next book in Nichole Severn's Blackhawk Security series.
Rules in Defiance *is available next month!*

An ear-piercing scream had Elliot Dunham reaching for the Glock stashed under his pillow. He threw back the sheets and pumped his legs hard, not bothering to check the time as the apartment blurred in his vision. That scream hadn't come from his apartment, but it had been close. Air rushed from his lungs as adrenaline burned through his veins. There was only one name that came to mind. "Waylynn."

Ripping open his front door, he made the sharp turn to his left in the darkness and faced his neighbor's front door. No hesitation. He aimed the heel of his foot toward the lock and kicked with everything he had. Pain shot up his leg, but the door splintered, thick wood slamming back against the wall. He raised the gun and moved in. One breath. Two. Nothing but the pounding of his heartbeat behind his ears registered. He scanned the scene, his senses adjusting slowly.

He'd gone into plenty of situations like this before, but this wasn't just another one of his clients. This was Waylynn. She mattered. He'd trained with Blackhawk Security, offered his clients personal protection, home security and investigative services as well as tactical training, wilderness survival and self-defense. But none of that would do Elliot a damn bit of good now. He was running off instinct. Because when it came to that woman, he couldn't think. Couldn't breathe.

Debris cut into his bare feet as he moved deeper into the dark apartment. A broken picture frame—Waylynn's doctorate degree from Texas A&M University—crunched beneath his weight. Torn couch cushions, a broken vase, a purse that'd been dumped over the floor. Signs of an obvious struggle littered the living room, but it was the trail of dark liquid leading to the back bedroom that homed his attention on the soft sobs echoing down the hallway. Blood. "Waylynn? It's Elliot. Are you dead?"

"Don't come in here!" That voice. Her voice.

"I take it that's a no." While his gut twisted at the hint of fear in her voice, relief spread through him. She was alive. And the scream...

Something horrible had happened to make her scream like that. The front door had been locked. No breeze came through the apartment from a broken window. Elliot moved down the hallway, putting his survival skills, which had been engrained into him since he was fourteen, to good use. No sign of a break-in. No movement from an intruder. He hit the bedroom and pushed on the partially open door with his free hand. The bed had been perfectly made, brightly colored throw pillows straight. Not much damage in this room. Light from beneath the closed bathroom door stretched across the beige carpeting.

And Elliot froze.

The gun faltered in his grip as water seeped from beneath the bathroom door. Not just water. Water mixed with blood. He shot forward. "I don't care if you're naked, doc. I'm coming in."

Elliot shouldered his way into the brightly lit bathroom and caught sight of his next-door neighbor huddled against the wall. Ice worked through him as he took in her soaked long blond hair, her stained oversize sweater and ripped black leggings, the terrified panic in her light blue eyes as she stared up at him, openmouthed.

And the dead woman in the bathtub.

"Oh, didn't realize this was a party." A hollow sensation carved itself into the pit of his stomach as he dropped the gun to his side. Terror etched deep lines around her mouth. Pressure built behind his sternum. Elliot set the gun on the counter and crouched in front of her, hands raised. Mildly aware he wore nothing but a pair of sweatpants, he ignored the urge to reach out for her. He'd take it slow. The woman in front of him wasn't the one he'd moved next door to a year ago. This wasn't the woman who'd caught his attention with a single smile and a six-pack of beer in her hand when she'd made the effort to introduce herself to her new neighbor. This woman was scared, vulnerable. Dangerous.

"Who's your friend?" he asked.

Her gaze wandered to the body, far too distant, far too empty. Color drained from her face. "Alexis."

"Okay, then. First piece of the mystery solved." Elliot framed her chin between his thumb and index finger and softened his voice. He didn't have a whole lot of training when it came to trauma victims, but he couldn't keep himself from touching her. "Second question. Are you the one bleeding?"

"I'm…" She turned that ice-blue gaze back

to him, her voice dropping into hollow territory. "I'm not the one bleeding."

"Now we're getting somewhere." He lowered his hand, careful of where he stepped, careful not to leave prints. He'd barged into the middle of an active crime scene. A crime scene where the most trusting woman he'd known stood in the center. There'd been a struggle, that much was clear. Things had obviously gotten out of hand, but he needed to hear the rest from her. He'd learned to trust his instincts a long time ago, and something about the scene, about Waylynn's scream a few minutes ago, didn't sit right. He pointed to the bathtub. "Last question. Why is there a dead woman in your tub?"

"I don't remember. It's all a blur. I woke up facedown on the bathroom floor. Water and—" she shuddered, wrapping her arms tighter around her middle "—blood were spilling over the edge of the bathtub. I got up and then I saw her. I screamed." Tears streamed down her cheeks and she wiped at them with the back of her long, thin fingers. She worked to swallow, her knees pressed against her chest, hands shaking. She blinked against the brightness of the lighting. "It's Alexis. Alexis Jacobs. She's my assistant at the lab."

Genism Corporation's lab. The largest, most profitable biotech company in Alaska. Also one of the military's biggest prospects for genetic testing, from what Elliot had learned, because Dr. Waylynn Hargraves herself had put them on the map. Advancing their research by decades according to recent publicity, she'd proven the existence of something called the warrior gene, a strand of DNA that ultimately predicted violent behavior.

Elliot scanned the scene again. Her research would've come in use right about now.

He dragged his thumb along her cheekbone, focused entirely on the size of her pupils and not the fact that every hair on the back of his neck had risen at the feel of her. Only a thin line of blue remained in her irises, which meant one of two things in a room this well lit. Either Waylynn had suffered a head injury during an altercation or she'd been drugged. Or both. He scanned down the long column of her throat. And found exactly what he was looking for. A tiny pinprick on the left side of her neck. The right size for a hypodermic needle. He exhaled hard. Damn it. She'd been drugged, made to look like she'd gone berserk on her assistant and then framed. "What's the last thing you remember?"

Anything to give them an idea of who'd done this. Because it sure as hell hadn't been Waylynn.

She blinked against the bathroom lights as though the brightness hurt. "I… I was supposed to meet Alexis here, at my apartment. She said she'd found something alarming in the recent study I oversaw at work, but she didn't want to discuss it over the phone or at the lab. She insisted on somewhere private where we couldn't be overheard."

If Waylynn had headed that study, anything alarming her assistant uncovered would've fallen back on her, threatened the project. But not if Alexis disappeared first. Whoever'd killed the assistant had known she and Waylynn were meeting and had planned the perfect setup, pinning his next-door neighbor as a murderer.

"Okay. You had a meeting scheduled here," he said. "You obviously got in your car and left the lab. Then what?"

"I—don't remember." She wrapped her fingers around his arms. "Elliot, why can't I remember?"

"Sorry to be the one to tell you this, doc, but I think you were drugged." He pointed at the faint angry puckered skin at the base of her throat to distract himself from the grip she had around his arms. "Hypodermic needle mark on the left side of your neck."

"There're only a handful of sedatives that affect memory. Benzodiazepines mostly. We store them at the lab." Hand automatically gravitating to the mark, she ran her fingertips over the abrasion. Her bottom lip parted from the top, attracting his attention to her mouth. That wide gaze wandered back to the tub, which absolutely destroyed her expression. Waylynn worked over sixty hours a week at the lab. Stood to reason her assistant did, too. They'd probably spent a lot of time together, gotten close. Shock smoothed the lines around her eyes. Her hands shook as she covered her mouth. "But drugging me doesn't explain how Alexis… This can't be happening. Not again."

Again? Alarm bells echoed in his head and his fight instinct clawed through him. "You know, that makes me think you killed somebody in a past life I don't know about."

Movement registered from somewhere inside the apartment, and Elliot reached for the gun on the counter. The metal warmed in his hand as he barricaded the door with his back.

Voices thundered through the apartment. Then footsteps outside the bathroom door. "Anchorage PD! We received a disturbance call from one of your neighbors. Is anyone here?" a distinct feminine voice asked.

"I don't know about you, but I haven't had this much excitement since getting shot at a few months ago." This night was getting better by the minute, yet Waylynn hadn't moved. "I don't mean to alarm you, doc, but I think the police are here. And they're probably going to arrest you."

"Elliot, I think I killed her." Waylynn's fingernails dug into his arms harder. "I think I killed Alexis."

Get 4 FREE REWARDS!

We'll send you 2 FREE Books plus 2 FREE Mystery Gifts.

Harlequin Presents® books feature a sensational and sophisticated world of international romance where sinfully tempting heroes ignite passion.

FREE Value Over $20

Get 4 FREE REWARDS!

We'll send you 2 FREE Books plus 2 FREE Mystery Gifts.

FREE
Value Over
$20

Both the **Romance** and **Suspense** collections feature compelling novels
written by many of today's bestselling authors.

YES! Please send me 2 FREE novels from the Essential Romance or
Essential Suspense Collection and my 2 FREE gifts (gifts are worth about
$10 retail). After receiving them, if I don't wish to receive any more books,
I can return the shipping statement marked "cancel." If I don't cancel, I will
receive 4 brand-new novels every month and be billed just $6.99 each in the
U.S. or $7.24 each in Canada. That's a savings of at least 13% off the cover
price. It's quite a bargain! Shipping and handling is just 50¢ per book in the
U.S. and $1.25 per book in Canada.* I understand that accepting the 2 free
books and gifts places me under no obligation to buy anything. I can always
return a shipment and cancel at any time. The free books and gifts are mine
to keep no matter what I decide.

Choose one: ☐ **Essential Romance**   ☐ **Essential Suspense**
          (194/394 MDN GNNP)   (191/391 MDN GNNP)

Name (please print)

Address   Apt. #

City   State/Province   Zip/Postal Code

Mail to the **Reader Service:**
IN U.S.A.: P.O. Box 1341, Buffalo, NY 14240-8531
IN CANADA: P.O. Box 603, Fort Erie, Ontario L2A 5X3

Want to try 2 free books from another series? Call 1-800-873-8635 or visit www.ReaderService.com.

*Terms and prices subject to change without notice. Prices do not include sales taxes, which will be charged (if applicable) based
on your state or country of residence. Canadian residents will be charged applicable taxes. Offer not valid in Quebec. This offer is
limited to one order per household. Books received may not be as shown. Not valid for current subscribers to the Essential Romance
or Essential Suspense Collection. All orders subject to approval. Credit or debit balances in a customer's account(s) may be offset by
any other outstanding balance owed by or to the customer. Please allow 4 to 6 weeks for delivery. Offer available while quantities last.

Your Privacy—The Reader Service is committed to protecting your privacy. Our Privacy Policy is available online at
www.ReaderService.com or upon request from the Reader Service. We make a portion of our mailing list available to reputable
third parties that offer products we believe may interest you. If you prefer that we not exchange your name with third parties, or if
you wish to clarify or modify your communication preferences, please visit us at www.ReaderService.com/consumerschoice or write
to us at Reader Service Preference Service, P.O. Box 9062, Buffalo, NY 14240-9062. Include your complete name and address.

STRS20

THE FORTUNES OF TEXAS COLLECTION!

18 FREE BOOKS in all!

Treat yourself to the rich legacy of the Fortune and Mendoza clans in this remarkable 50-book collection. This collection is packed with cowboys, tycoons and Texas-sized romances!

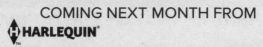
INTRIGUE

Available November 19, 2019

#1893 SAFETY BREACH
Longview Ridge Ranch • by Delores Fossen
Former profiler Gemma Hanson is in witness protection, but she's still haunted by memories of the serial killer who tried to kill her last year. Her concerns skyrocket when Sheriff Kellan Slater tells her the murderer has learned her location and is coming to finish what he started.

#1894 UNDERCOVER ACCOMPLICE
Red, White and Built: Delta Force Deliverance
by Carol Ericson
When Delta Force soldier Hunter Mancini learns the group that kidnapped CIA operative Sue Chandler is now framing his team leader, he asks for her help. But could she be hiding something that would clear his boss?

#1895 AMBUSHED AT CHRISTMAS
Rushing Creek Crime Spree • by Barb Han
After a jogger resembling Detective Leah Cordon is murdered, rancher Deacon Kent approaches her, believing the attack is related to recent cattle mutilations. Can they find the killer before he corners Leah?

#1896 DANGEROUS CONDITIONS
Protectors at Heart • by Jenna Kernan
Former soldier Logan Lynch's first investigation as the constable of a small town leads him to microbiologist Paige Morris, whose boss was killed. Yet as they search for the murderer, Paige is forced to reveal a secret that shows the stakes couldn't be higher.

#1897 RULES IN DEFIANCE
Blackhawk Security • by Nichole Severn
Blackhawk Security investigator Elliot Dunham never expected his neighbor to show up bruised and covered in blood in the middle of the night. To protect Waylynn Hargraves, Elliot must defy the rules he's set for himself, because he knows he's all that stands between her and certain death.

#1898 HIDDEN TRUTH
Stealth • by Danica Winters
When undercover CIA agent Trevor Martin meets Sabrina Parker, the housekeeper at the ranch where he's lying low, he doesn't know she's an undercover FBI agent. After a murder on the property, the operatives must work together, but can they discover their hidden connection before it's too late?

YOU CAN FIND MORE INFORMATION ON UPCOMING HARLEQUIN® TITLES, FREE EXCERPTS AND MORE AT WWW.HARLEQUIN.COM.

HICNM1119